"Now Aren't You Glad You Came?"

Warren teased.

"Oh, I am. I wouldn't have missed this meal for the world."

"Meal?" he asked, pretending to be offended. "What about the company?"

Meredith's laugh echoed over the lapping waves of the river. "Now, really, you were so busy enjoying your dinner that you didn't even notice I was here."

For just a second there was a flash of fire in Warren's eyes. Softly he murmured, "It wouldn't take long to prove you wrong about that."

KATE MERIWETHER
lives in Texas and is the mother of three sons. She wrote *Sweet Adversity,* her first Silhouette, during her second year of law school and will be graduating a month after it is published.

Dear Reader:

Silhouette has always tried to give you exactly what you want. When you asked for increased realism, deeper characterization and greater length, we brought you Silhouette Special Editions. When you asked for increased sensuality, we brought you Silhouette Desire. Now you ask for books with the length and depth of Special Editions, the sensuality of Desire, but with something else besides, something that no one else offers. Now we bring you SILHOUETTE INTIMATE MOMENTS, true romance novels, longer than the usual, with all the depth that length requires. More sensuous than the usual, with characters whose maturity matches that sensuality. Books with the ingredient no one else has tapped: excitement.

There is an electricity between two people in love that makes everything they do magic, larger than life—and this is what we bring you in SILHOUETTE INTIMATE MOMENTS. Look for them this May, wherever you buy books.

These books are for the woman who wants more than she has ever had before. These books are for you. As always, we look forward to your comments and suggestions. You can write to me at the address below:

Karen Solem
Editor-in-Chief
Silhouette Books
P.O. Box 769
New York, N.Y. 10019

KATE MERIWETHER

Sweet Adversity

Published by Silhouette Books New York

America's Publisher of Contemporary Romance

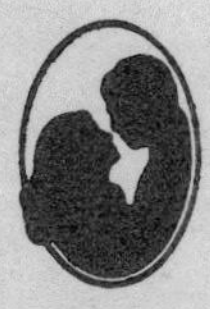

SILHOUETTE BOOKS, a Simon & Schuster Division of
GULF & WESTERN CORPORATION
1230 Avenue of the Americas, New York, N.Y. 10020

Distributed by Pocket Books

ISBN: 0-671-53589-7

First Silhouette Books printing April, 1983

10 9 8 7 6 5 4 3 2 1

Map by Ray Lundgren

America's Publisher of Contemporary Romance

Printed in the U.S.A.

To
Candace Camp
for her interest and her example

and to
my law-school friends
for their encouragement

Sweet Adversity

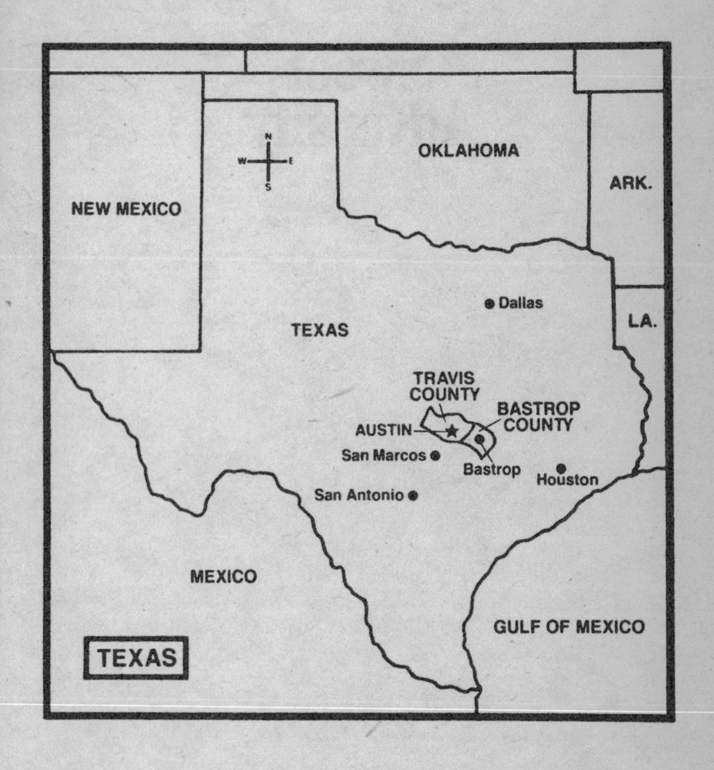
OKLAHOMA
NEW MEXICO
ARK.
N
W
E
S
Dallas
LA.
TEXAS
TRAVIS
COUNTY
BASTROP
COUNTY
AUSTIN
San Marcos
Bastrop
Houston
San Antonio
MEXICO
GULF OF MEXICO
TEXAS

Chapter One

Harvey Gilstrap attempted to hurry his generous girth down the corridor of the Adult Probation Office, a perplexed frown on his normally cheerful face. With a shiny-domed head bordered by a mere fringe of hair and dimples that worked in his plump, rosy cheeks, he needed nothing more than a halo to be mistaken for an overweight cherub. When he roared, however, he was as easily mistaken for a grizzly bear—though the probation officers whom he supervised knew that his bluster was purely for effect.

"Meredith, drop everything," Harvey squeezed his frame through the door to her small office, oblivious of the tired-looking probationer who sat across the desk from Meredith.

"I'll be with you in just a second, Harvey. We're almost finished." Meredith pushed her blonde hair back out of her eyes and attempted to ignore Harvey long enough to finish jotting down the details of the woman's monthly probation visit: yes, she was working every day; no, she wasn't drinking any more; yes, she had made the payment on her fine. Meredith gave the woman a smile of encouragement and tried not to feel frustrated because she sometimes spent more time on departmental paperwork than she did actually helping the probationers who were assigned to her. A side glance at Harvey's distressed face made Meredith hurry the woman out of the tiny cubicle and give her undivided attention to her impatient supervisor.

"Is something wrong?" she asked, her voice soft. When Harvey was upset, it was best to calm him.

"As usual, everything happens at once." Harvey slumped into the brown vinyl chair which the probationer had just vacated and poked a file folder at Meredith. "I have an appointment with Judge Baxter at three o'clock to discuss the pre-sentence report on Diego Gutierrez. And the sheriff's office just called to say they've picked up one of our probationers on an armed robbery. I've got to get over to the jail right away." Harvey sighed, feeling sorry for himself and his burdens as chief supervisor of the Travis County Adult Probation Department.

Multiple crises were a way of life for probation officers, and after four years Meredith had learned to live with the perpetual havoc, remaining cheerful despite what some would consider the dreariness of the work. But it was never dreary to Meredith. She felt she had an important role to play in salvaging the lives of people who would otherwise be in prison. "What would you like me to do? I can run over to the jail and interview the defendant for you," she offered.

"No, I need to do that myself. It will help me more if you'll keep my appointment with Judge Baxter." Harvey's eyes slid away from Meredith's direct gaze.

"Harvey, you chicken," she sputtered in irritation. "Ever since you transferred me to the central office you've talked about how Judge Baxter wants to throw everybody in prison and toss away the key. How can you do this to me?"

"Easy." Harvey almost chuckled until he saw the sparks blazing in Meredith's eyes. "Now, Meredith. Diego Gutierrez is your probationer. You're the one who knows him. Maybe *you* can convince the judge that he deserves another chance. Lord only knows you convinced me."

"Diego does deserve another chance. He's just a mixed-up kid. I don't think prison will accomplish anything for him." Meredith leaned forward, her small fist pounding the desk in emphasis.

"Then explain that to the judge. Maybe he'll listen to you."

"Fat chance." Meredith had heard quite enough about Judge Baxter. Stern and unyielding, the judge had first been elected to the bench six years ago on a law-and-order platform, and so far almost every defendant who appeared before him had been sentenced to the state penitentiary. Only rarely had the judge granted probation. Meredith felt a sense of futility. Poor Diego. Why couldn't Judge Baxter understand that there were *two* sides to criminal justice, rehabilitation as well as punishment?

Meredith believed it was vitally important to rehabilitate criminal defendants so they could make a contribution to society instead of being a burden. Four years as a probation officer had done nothing to diminish Meredith's idealism. Her work was her life, her consuming passion, and all her considerable energy went into planning new strategies and programs to reach those persons branded "criminal" by society. She had the zeal of a crusader because she believed in her work. She was the best probation officer in Travis County, but she was too modest to realize it.

Harvey tossed the well-worn file onto Meredith's desk. "You've got ten minutes to review the file and get over to the judge's chambers," he said. "You believe in Diego. If you can't convince the judge, nobody can. Give it your best shot." Harvey rose and lumbered out of the office. "Meanwhile, I'll get over to the jail and see if I can straighten out that problem."

Meredith gave Harvey a dirty look. "Harvey, all I can say is, there *better* be one of your probationers at the jail. If this is one of your trumped-up stories, so help me, you're going to be opening a criminal file on me—for *homicide.*"

This time Harvey really did hurry his 253 pounds down the hallway. He grabbed his hat from the rack in the lobby and darted out the front door, puffing.

Meredith sat in the reception area outside the judge's office and wondered why she had bothered to hurry across Guadalupe Street. His Honor was "detained" while Meredith cooled her heels in his waiting room. She brushed imaginary flecks off her navy linen suit, glad that she had worn something tailored and professional to work today. She had never been involved in a presentence interview with a judge before, and she felt a little nervous. Actually, more than a little—her mouth was dry and her palms were sweating. She hoped she wouldn't have to shake hands. She reached in her leather bag for a tissue and tried to wipe her hands without the judge's secretary seeing her. Thin-lipped and straight-backed, Miss Tuttle was quite intimidating.

The county courthouse was its usual hustle and bustle, with lawyers, jurors and witnesses wandering the corridors during the afternoon recess. There were five courtrooms on the third floor of the courthouse, and all of them seemed to have trials going on. During the afternoon recess, while jurors were having a cigarette or getting a drink of water, most of the judges took time for a cup of coffee and relaxed for a few minutes. But not Judge Baxter—*he* scheduled appointments. Another appointment had already been ushered into chambers before Meredith arrived. No wonder Judge Baxter was so stern, Meredith thought. He drove himself and probably everyone around him. Certainly his secretary looked like a perpetual-motion machine as she pounded the typewriter rapid-fire.

Meredith's nervousness gave way to anger. How did Judge Baxter expect her to give him an adequate report when he scheduled two appointments in one fifteen-minute recess? She needed time to explain Diego's predicament. *Time!* She'd be lucky if she got ten minutes—Meredith glanced at her watch—or even five. She bent her head in concentration, trying to organize the information on Diego's background so she could present it quickly and effectively.

"Miss Jennings, the judge will see you now," the secretary interrupted. Her voice was cold and crisp, without a trace of the Southern warmth which was usually the norm in Austin, Texas.

Meredith had been so absorbed in her thoughts that she had not noticed the departure of the previous visitor. She looked up in time to catch a glimpse of Judge Baxter, robes swirling as he bade goodbye to an extremely attractive woman. Meredith recognized her at once—Bettis Langley, anchorwoman for one of the Austin television stations. She and the judge seemed to be old friends . . . or something more, if their warm exchange of glances meant anything. One last smile and Bettis Langley walked past Meredith, the scent of expensive perfume trailing behind her. Meredith glanced down at her navy linen suit again. All at once it seemed drab.

"Miss Jennings, *please,* this way," the secretary said, her voice a reprimand. Apparently dawdling was not permitted in Miss Tuttle's efficient and well-ordered world.

Meredith rose, propelled by necessity, her thoughts suddenly churning. As a candidate for state district judge, Judge Baxter had been pictured on billboards around Austin. Meredith had noticed them as well as his many television ads. She had even seen him occasionally in person—across the street or down the hall, but she had never seen him up close before. His teeming animal energy came as a shock to her because he had a vitality that had not been captured in the photographs.

Bursting with health, tanned by playing year-round tennis, Judge Baxter in his black robes looked like the original fallen angel. Lucifer himself probably had the same mischievous glint in his eye. Meredith stepped toward Judge Baxter thinking that he certainly had the aura of power; it emanated from him just as the perfume had floated around Bettis Langley. Meredith had never been exposed to the sexuality of raw power before, and she felt confused, tongue-tied. The man's magnetism had driven all thought of Diego Gutierrez from her mind.

Judge Baxter was quite aware of his effect. He grinned. "And who are you?" he asked. "My appointment book says Harvey Gilstrap should be standing here right now. But you don't look a thing like Harvey." The judge's eyes appraised Meredith with interest. There was nothing lascivious in his look, yet there was a kind of . . . *knowing* in it. She had never felt more female. Her breath quickened, and she stammered a bit as she mechanically offered her right hand.

"I'm Meredith Jennings. Harvey had an emergency and asked me to keep this appointment for him." Judge Baxter's handshake was warm and firm, his gaze direct. Meredith's stomach did somersaults. She clutched the file folder in her left hand and wondered what to say next. Surely she shouldn't keep staring into his—what color eyes? dark, so dark, with glints of gold and laughter—or she would lose her balance.

"Well?" Judge Baxter waited impatiently for Meredith to continue. "What is it? It's unusual for a probation officer to request an appointment this way. Have you written your report and recommendation?"

Apparently there were two men standing in front of Meredith rather than the one who was visible to her. One of them had laughing eyes that teased her, dared her to take his measure as a man; the other was strictly business, urging her to get to the point. Meredith became even more confused. Damn Harvey, anyway, throwing her to the lions this way! She didn't have the job experience to cope with a judge who was only too aware of the power of his office . . . and of his effect on women. Meredith drew a deep breath and tried to clear her head.

"Yes, Your Honor. The report is here, but there are extenuating circumstances in this case, and we felt the written report should be supplemented with an oral report."

"Miss Jennings, I'm in the middle of a trial and time is short. Haven't you been a probation officer long enough to know that there are extenuating circumstances in *every* case?" There was sarcasm in his voice, and Meredith remembered Judge Baxter's reputation for tough sentences.

"Of course I have. But Diego Gutierrez is even more—"

"Look, I don't have the time or the patience to listen to some sob story. And tell Harvey he might as well come himself the next time. It won't work for him to send an attractive female to—"

The telephone shrilled. Judge Baxter excused himself and spoke briefly to his secretary. He glanced at his watch, then at the file folder in Meredith's hand. "Tell him I'll be right with him," he said into the receiver. Turning back to Meredith, he said, "Sorry, Miss Jennings, but George Rockwell is outside and I'll have to see him before I go back into the courtroom."

Meredith couldn't believe that the judge was actually going to terminate the interview like this. So what if George Rockwell was front-runner in the gubernatorial race and had turned up on the judge's doorstep? Meredith was a supporter of Rockwell and wanted him to be elected, but not at the expense of poor Diego Gutierrez, who desperately needed his day in court. Anger drove all caution from Meredith's mind. "No doubt Mr. Rockwell wants to get some campaign advice from a real *winner,*" she said, her voice edged with bitterness. "Never mind the poor jerk who actually expects the criminal justice system to dispense *justice.*"

"Just a minute there, Miss High and Mighty," Judge Baxter answered, nettled by her remark. "Will the world come to an end if this conference is postponed?"

"Diego is scheduled to be sentenced at nine o'clock in the morning. 'Later' will be *too* late for him." Meredith mentally kicked herself for wasting the precious few minutes at the beginning when she should have been making her pitch instead of fawning like an adolescent schoolgirl. She squared her shoulders and started for the door.

"Hold on, now, and let me think before you go off in such a huff." The judge wrinkled his brow. "I'll be in court until five, so the rest of the afternoon is out. Tell you what, I'll buy you a drink after work and you can tell me the whole sad story about your dear Diego. How's that for a consolation prize?"

How could one man be so maddening? And why did he taunt her with that impish grin? She recognized the challenge in his eyes. There was something about him that made Meredith feel frightened—not of him, but of herself. Her emotions were helter-skelter. She was out of her depth, and she knew it. Best to say no. She had almost begun to shake her head when she remembered Diego. If she blew this chance, he would go to the penitentiary for sure, and he would go tomorrow. She had to fight for him. He had nobody else. "Thanks," she answered, suddenly changing her mind. Her voice came out annoyingly soft. "It really means a lot to me. I'd like to help Diego get a fair shake."

"Wait for me outside the Stokes Building. I'll pick

you up on the corner at 5:15." With characteristic firmness Judge Baxter steered Meredith out the door, pausing long enough to introduce her to George "Rocky" Rockwell, then warmly ushering the political candidate into his office, "but only for a minute, Rocky, I'm due back in the courtroom in three minutes."

The rest of the afternoon was a lost cause for Meredith. She couldn't concentrate and did almost nothing but sit at her desk staring at a file folder, her heart filled alternately with dread and anticipation. At 5:10 she took the elevator down and stood in the October sun, enjoying the lovely Texas day. Behind her was the Stokes Building where she worked, a five-story office building which was utilitarian and devoid of glamour. It was, however, ideally located for the agencies which had been crowded out of the courthouse across the street with the gradual expansion of county government. Diagonally across the busy street stood the Travis County Courthouse, a fifty-year-old building of the same Cordova cream limestone which had been popular for many of the buildings in this area. Adjoining the courthouse to the south was Wooldridge Square, a historic park—a green oasis with stately live oaks, sycamores, and pecan trees which flourished in the midst of cement and traffic.

Promptly at 5:15 P.M. a silver Mercedes pulled out of the heavy traffic to the curb and tooted its horn, and Meredith felt strangely self-conscious getting inside with a man who no longer wore his judicial robes, who was, in fact, loosening his tie and removing his suit jacket while she got inside. "I should have helped with the door, I suppose," he said, though he did not seem at all apologetic. "But this is business. Chivalry and business don't seem to mix." He smiled at her. "However it's after hours. Call me Warren. And I'll call you—"

"Meredith."

"Yes. I checked." Again he gave her that appraising look, and she knew that he was aware of every aspect of her femininity. Well, she had checked on him, too. Thirty-six years old, graduate of the University of Texas law school, tops in his class, former district attorney in Bastrop County, oil money in the family. And single. Never married. Meredith's eyes lowered to her hands, folded demurely in her lap. She better not look at him. It made her heart do crazy things.

The Mercedes rolled easily down the Austin streets in the five o'clock traffic, turning off Burnet onto West North Loop. "How about Fonda San Miguel?" Warren asked. "They have good marguerita, and we can talk there."

Fonda San Miguel was one of the most romantic restaurants in Austin, with its carved wooden doors, Mexican wrought-iron chandeliers, and lush tropical foliage. There was even a parrot. It was one of Meredith's favorite places, but she had the feeling that Warren was not really asking permission to take her there. He had decided, and all that remained was for her to ratify his decision. He was used to taking charge; Meredith felt a strange lethargy and was willing to let him do so. Normally strong-willed herself, she sensed his stronger will and for the moment was willing to be swept along in the company of dark eyes, black hair, and an engaging grin. She murmured assent and leaned back in the leather cushion, wondering how the evening would progress.

* * *

Meredith and Warren sipped frosty margaritas in tall, stemmed glasses rimmed with salt, and it wasn't long before Meredith felt the tequila make her a little light-headed and dizzy. "I think we'd better get down to business while I can still think," she murmured. She looked around for Diego's file and found it propped against her purse in the empty chair next to her.

"There's no hurry," Warren answered. "I don't have another engagement until eight o'clock. How about another drink?" His glass was empty and his eyes were as clear as ever.

"Not for me, thanks. I can't drink much on an empty stomach. Makes me giddy."

"I'll order a plate of *botanas* for you," Warren said, signaling their waiter. "I'd buy your dinner, but I already have a dinner engagement." He paused, then added, "With Bettis Langley. She's looking for an angle on a story about the Texas criminal justice system since that's become an issue in the gubernatorial race."

"It always makes it nice for a reporter to have such excellent inside sources for news stories," Meredith answered, as lightly as she could. She silently vowed she would never watch Channel 36 again.

"Bettis is a damn good reporter, too good for a town as small as Austin. I don't know how Channel 36 has managed to keep her this long." Warren seemed to appreciate Bettis's talents. And of course the woman was good. Everybody talked about Bettis Langley's ability to get the best from her interview subjects. She could set them at ease so they talked to the camera as easily as to an old friend.

What on earth are we doing talking about Bettis Langley? Meredith wondered glumly. It was depressing to hear Warren praise another woman. All the sparkle had gone out of the evening. She lifted her eyes to find Warren studying her with an enigmatic expression. She had the feeling he could read her thoughts and that he understood her better than she understood herself. For heavens sake, why should she feel jealous about a woman she had never seen in person until this afternoon? What difference did it make that this man sitting next to her spoke affectionately about a talented and attractive woman? None, absolutely none. Meredith decided to have another drink to dull the inexplicable ache in her heart and realized that she had somehow managed to amuse Warren very much.

Apparently satisfied that he had her attention, Warren leaned back and began to draw Meredith into conversation. Soon she found herself talking easily to him, telling him about her childhood in Houston. Meredith had worked her way through the University of Houston and earned a degree in criminal justice, then worked for a year with the Houston probation department. But she hadn't liked the city, which grew more rapidly with each passing year, and finally Meredith knew she had to get away to a more serene environment. She had been grateful to get a job in Austin, where the competition for good jobs was always fierce. Austin was a charming town, with a youth-oriented, casual attitude—not laid back in the California style, but in a unique Southern way. It had the political excitement of being the state capital and was big enough to offer many of the advantages of a metropolitan area, yet small enough to have a real home-town atmosphere.

Meredith told Warren about the little house she had bought her first year in Austin. She had refinished the hardwood floors, grouted the casement windows, and tended the honeysuckle and azaleas that grew beside the front porch. Meredith had found peace in Austin and a sense of purpose in her work. Her life was full and complete.

"And what about the men in your life?" Warren asked impudently. "Doesn't sound to me like you have much room for a man."

"Oh, well . . . there are men, of course. I date some pretty nice fellows." Meredith felt her throat tighten. Why did it make her nervous for Warren to ask about her boyfriends?

"One of the advantages of a job at the courthouse," he observed. "There are men everywhere."

"I don't think of my job that way," Meredith said, offended. "I'm a probation officer because I want to work with people in trouble and help them try to straighten out their lives."

"I'm sure your success rate is remarkable," he answered, his voice tinged with irony.

"Not great. But there are some successes. Sometimes the only thing people need is for somebody to believe in them, believe that they can change."

"Oh, sure. Like your dear Diego Gutierrez, I suppose?"

"Yes, like Diego. He's just a poor kid from the wrong side of town who never learned how to function in an Anglo world. It doesn't mean he's bad, or that he's dangerous to society. It just means he needs some help."

"As I recall, he's had several tickets for reckless driving and been arrested twice for breaking into coin boxes. Now he's stolen a car. And you say he's just a poor kid from the wrong side of town. He sounds to me like somebody who never learned to respect the rights or the property of other people."

"But can't you understand what it's like to be poor, and not speak English very well? He's never yet had a job that even paid the minimum wage. There are seven children in his family, and they've all worked since they were small. His grades were so bad he dropped out of school at sixteen, as soon as the law would let him. He's never even had a chance."

"How old is he now, Meredith? Seventeen? Eighteen?" Warren's voice held a challenge. He already knew the answer.

"He's twenty-four."

"He's not just a kid, Meredith. How long are you going to make excuses for him?"

"I have to disagree with you. It's not a question of making excuses. Poverty and illiteracy—those things are real to people like Diego. They're forces beyond his control and are the *reasons* for his behavior. We asked for an appointment with you so we could explain what hap—"

Warren interrupted impatiently. "I'm sorry, but it's a little hard for me to accept the idea that a 24-year-old man—*man,* not kid—doesn't have to be accountable for his actions just like anybody else."

Meredith tried her best to be firm and reasonable. "Will you just let me explain—"

Warren turned obstinate. "The defendant will get his chance to explain for himself—in open court."

Meredith's heart sunk in dismay. Diego's future was at stake and she was losing the battle. Desperation drove her to greater lengths. "You don't understand. You'll never understand," she said, annoyed that her voice was trembling. "How can you? You've had all the advantages—money, brains, family connections, looks. You don't have the faintest idea what it's like to be in Diego's shoes—or bare feet, most of the time."

They glared at each other over the plate of cold *botanas.* Gone now were the sparks of electricity that had sizzled between them. Their minds were engaged in a contest of wills, each stubbornly locked in opposing positions.

"Diego got arrested, and they didn't have the money for a lawyer. The state appointed a lawyer, but the family didn't have the money for his bond, so he went to jail. He's still in jail. His family could barely make it with his paycheck, and now they've lost that. They'll have to go on welfare. If he were put on probation, I could get him in a vocational training program—auto mechanics, maybe—so he would have a chance to make a decent wage and have something to hope for. He doesn't need to be thrown in prison to teach him a lesson. He's had enough lessons. What he needs is training and a decent job. He's no threat to society, and it's cheaper for the state to put him to work than to put him in prison."

Meredith had talked with rising breath, impassioned but managing to keep her voice under control. She had said too much. She knew that. But she couldn't help herself. It was so important. She had thought if she could just make Warren understand, then he wouldn't be so hard on Diego. But it was impossible. Warren's kind, born to privilege, could never understand. She pushed her soft, blonde hair out of her eyes and rose. "Sorry I got on my soapbox," she said, tears misting her eyes. "Would you take me back to the office? You have an appointment, and I need to work."

They drove back downtown in silence. Warren had

hardly said a word since Meredith had spoken. His lips were set in a stern line, and the laughter was gone from his eyes. Apparently women who were idealists did not amuse him at all. Meredith shrunk into her corner of the car and gave herself up to hateful thoughts until the Mercedes pulled into the parking garage next to the Stokes Building where she worked.

"Just let me out here," Meredith said.

"Which car is yours? No need to walk in the dark. I'll drive you over there."

"It's not necessary. This is fine. Thanks for the drink . . . and the exchange of philosophies."

Her sarcasm goaded him to a sharp retort. "I admire your idealism, but it won't work in the real world. Face it, Meredith. People like Diego aren't going to change."

Meredith jerked the door handle and got out of the car. His words affected her like a slap in the face, striking at everything she believed in. She could not get away from him fast enough.

"I said I'd see you to your car," Warren said, irritation in his voice.

"Business and chivalry don't mix, remember?" There was an edge of distress in her voice that surprised him. He got out and walked around the car, taking Meredith's arm in a strong grip. She could feel the warmth of his breath against her hair as he practically pushed her across the parking building. Again she had the feeling of being almost overpowered by his greater strength.

"Let me go," she cried. "I can walk without your pulling me." Embarrassed at her lack of control and aware that the tequila was making her vulnerable, she wanted to be rid of Warren and his effect on her. She broke away and hurried toward her battered Volkswagen, but he ran past and easily outdistanced her.

"I jog three miles every morning before breakfast," he said in a bantering tone when she caught up with him. He really had not meant to upset her, and in fact did not understand why it happened. He had never seen a probation officer who seemed so personally involved in a case. Obviously she was upset—he could sense the tension that tightened her body. He put a casual hand on her shoulder and felt the reflex that made her jerk away from him.

"Meredith, I don't know what happened. I didn't mean to upset you," he said with sincerity. She nodded, still averting her head. "I didn't mean for you to take my comments personally. We just have a different perspective, that's all."

"It's okay," she answered, digging unsuccessfully in her purse for her car keys.

"Are you sure?" he asked. There was still a suspicious sound in her voice. He reached out and tilted her head toward the dim light so he could see her expression. She felt a current almost like electricity pass through her at his touch, and she gazed up at him with tear-filled eyes. Something stirred in Warren, responding to the irresistible combination of attraction and compassion that emanated from her. For another moment he held her face in his hands, gazing into her liquid eyes, fighting the magnetism that flowed between them. Then his arms were around her, pulling her body close to his, melting into his, yearning, joining, warmth against warmth, his lips touching her hair, her cheek, her ear, then finding her lips with devastating effect. His heart hammered against her breast, and she could feel her own pulse throb at her temples. His hands stroked her hair, which fell loosely down her back, then gripped her shoulders and pulled her closer toward him. Again his head bent, his mouth searching, finding her mouth, tasting, probing with a sweetness like cherry wine. Meredith couldn't breathe, didn't want to. It would be enough to die here in his arms, so blissful that heaven itself could offer no more joy. She twined her arms around his neck and drew him deeper into the kiss, feeling his body surge against hers, feeling her own respond with an urgency she had never known before.

A horn honked behind Warren's Mercedes blocking the entry, and headlights bounced against the wall. "Hey, move your car," someone called.

"Damnation," he muttered, his arms reluctant to let her go. "Go away." His head bent again.

But Meredith was shocked into consciousness. The other car had come in the nick of time. What was she thinking of? How could she be so reckless as to end up in a passionate embrace with the very judge who would sentence her probationer tomorrow? She wasn't thinking, not at all—not of Diego, not of herself, not of her work. She had nearly lost her sanity. She did not dare look at Warren. Her response had been wanton and beyond her control. No doubt the amused expression was back on his face, now that he had demonstrated his power to arouse her sexually and divert her from her purpose. But he couldn't! She would resist him, for Diego and for all the others like him who needed her help.

Before Warren could say a word, Meredith snatched her keys out of her purse and unlocked the car door.

"What do you think you're doing?" he asked, reaching to kiss her again.

"I'm going home to work. You really must move your car, Judge Baxter, before it gets hit. Besides, you're going to be late for your dinner engagement . . . with Bettis Langley."

Chapter Two

Meredith slipped in the side door of the courtroom just before nine o'clock the next morning and seated herself at the end of an oak bench. Across from her, near the windows, Diego's family huddled at another bench. Diego's mother was crying softly, and anguished whispers in Spanish broke the somber silence. Thanks to intensive language study, Meredith could understand the whispers and sympathized with the family's anxiety. In front of the rail, near the judge's bench, sat Diego, dressed in an ill-fitting suit the jail had provided for his trip to the courtroom. Scott

Palmer, his court-appointed lawyer, sat beside him, pulling papers from a briefcase. A prosecutor from the district attorney's office sat at the other counsel table, and in the front of the courtroom the deputy clerk was arranging papers and the court reporter was setting up his equipment. It was almost time for court to begin. Meredith steeled herself for the worst. After last night, she had lost all hope.

Last night . . . when Warren had held her in his arms and she had clung to him, aching with desire. Last night, when she had been so foolish as to let her physical response to Warren Baxter distract her from her purpose in meeting him. Last night, when . . . Meredith shook her head. She had hardly slept, her brain tormented with these same thoughts. Somehow she must put Warren the man out of her mind and think of him only as a judge—*the* judge—the one who would sentence Diego in a few short minutes. Meredith massaged her aching temples. She had a splitting headache.

The bailiff called for order and everybody rose. Court was in session. Warren entered from the door at the front of the courtroom and strode to the bench with his black robe flowing around him.

"I call the case of *State* vs. *Gutierrez,*" Warren said, his voice crisp. "Is the defendant present in the courtroom?"

Scott Palmer rose, nudging Diego to stand beside him. "The defendant is present, Your Honor," Scott replied.

"Is the State ready to proceed with sentencing?"

The prosecutor rose. He was someone new to the district attorney's office, and Meredith did not recognize him. Probably a new law school graduate. "The

State is ready, Your Honor," the prosecutor replied, his voice quavering a little.

"I have examined the file on this defendant and given careful study to the report and recommendation of the Adult Probation Office." Warren shuffled through the file in front of him, his tanned fingers finding the paper he wanted. "I find that there are some questions in my mind as to the circumstances of this offense. Is the defendant willing to take the stand and respond under oath to questions put by the court?"

Scott Palmer looked puzzled and glanced at the prosecutor. This was somewhat unusual, but a prime rule for defense counsel was to "humor the judge." Scott whispered in Diego's ear and received a nod.

"Your Honor, the defendant is willing to testify. In all fairness to my client, however, I feel that I should inform the court that this defendant's English is not very good. Could we have an interpreter present?"

"Does the State agree that an interpreter is necessary to protect the defendant's rights?"

The poor young prosecutor didn't know what to say, but a prime rule for prosecutors was to "cover your ass," jokingly referred to in the district attorney's office as "C.Y.A." In his ears echoed all the admonitions of law school concerning cases which had been dismissed on appeal because of technical violations of the rights of defendants. He capitulated. "Yes, Your Honor."

"Very well. We will have a short recess while defense counsel obtains the services of an interpreter. Court will resume in thirty minutes." Warren rose, and the bailiff quickly cried, "All rise." By the time the spectators got to their feet, Warren was already out the door. Scott Palmer dashed out the side door, the prosecutor close behind.

What on earth was going on? Warren's courtroom had a reputation for well-oiled efficiency. Procedures of this kind were not the norm. Meredith started toward the counsel table to offer Diego some reassurance, but the bailiff who was supervising him looked unfriendly. Diego's family continued their whispering in frantic Spanish. Meredith could appreciate their anxiety in a situation that was so alien to them.

Scott came in the side door and approached Meredith. They were good friends, had dated off and on for two years, and knew each other well. Scott's appointment as Diego's counsel had assured her that Diego would receive the same careful attention as that of a paying client.

"Meredith, I need a favor," Scott said, his voice a whisper. "The regular interpreters are out of pocket and it will take nearly an hour to get one of them over here. Will you interpret for us?"

"Me?" Meredith had been pressed into such service before, but never for one of her own probationers. "I guess so, if it's okay with the judge."

"Good. I'll go ask him. Thanks." Scott hurried out the door and around to chambers, leaving Meredith wondering what might happen next. This was the strangest sentencing procedure she had ever experienced.

Within three minutes Scott was back, his face red. "Never mind, Meredith. Judge Baxter says he wants an impartial interpreter. I'll get someone else. We'll just have to wait."

Scott was gone before Meredith could react. Her face flamed crimson with fury. Did Warren actually believe that she would bias the translation in favor of Diego? Her integrity as a probation officer had never been questioned before, and to think that it would become suspect now, by Judge Warren Baxter of all people, stung her pride. She rose and started back to chambers to tell Warren how offended she was, but then her eyes fell on Diego, sitting with his head folded in his hands, and she slumped back into her seat. To call Warren to task would only hurt Diego's case. She couldn't do that. She gritted her teeth and waited.

The next hour was an eternity of churning thoughts and anxiety, but finally it ended and an interpreter arrived. Within moments people were in their proper places and Warren was back on the bench. Diego was sworn by the clerk and took the witness chair, his voice a frightened murmur which was amplified by the microphone. Warren was surprisingly accommodating in asking his questions, speaking slowly and in short pauses so that the interpreter would have time to translate accurately.

"Mr. Gutierrez, you have been found guilty of stealing an automobile belonging to someone else, and today you are to be sentenced for that crime."

Diego listened intently to the interpreter, then nodded his head.

"You'll have to answer out loud so the court reporter can write down your answer," Warren explained.

"Yes, Your Honor," Diego said, his fingers twisting nervously in his lap.

"I would like for you to tell me, under oath, why you stole the car."

A torrent of Spanish escaped Diego's lips, and the interpreter struggled briefly, then gave up in defeat. Realizing that something was wrong, Diego stopped and started over, more slowly, though sometimes he still got ahead of the interpreter. He explained that his younger sister Rosita had a boyfriend who had gone to the Valley to hunt for work in the fruit groves. After her boyfriend left, Rosita discovered that she was pregnant. She needed to go to the Valley to find her boyfriend so they could get married.

A bus ticket to Harlingen cost $25, but they did not have that much money. Rosita cried all day and all night, and Diego had to help her, so he stole a car to drive her the 300 miles. But they were arrested before they ever got to San Marcos.

Diego turned and looked into the judge's eyes. He stopped speaking Spanish and spoke very slow English.

"Me, I was arrested and took to jail. My sister, she go home but nobody could help her. So she go to the free clinic and she get rid of the baby. Then my sister, she feel so guilty that the Blessed Virgin punish her. So Rosita, she cry and cry and nobody can help her. Now I go to jail, and there nobody to help nobody."

Warren had listened intently, his face impassive. It was impossible for Meredith to know what he was thinking. She supposed Warren was used to human heartbreak and steeled himself against it, the way doctors have to steel themselves against suffering in order to continue practicing medicine.

Silence hung over the courtroom, all eyes fixed upon the judge to see what he would do. Yet Warren seemed able to block out the expectant audience and withdraw into himself to ponder Diego's fate, unruffled and unhurried. Meredith had never seen such composure. The part of her that could think of Warren as judge rather than as man found him climbing several notches in her estimation. She admired cool professionalism, and though she strove for it herself, her emotions often got entangled.

At last Warren broke the silence. "Mr. Gutierrez, I had intended to sentence you to a year in prison, based on your past record and the present offense. It is a very serious matter to take property that belongs to another person, do you understand that?"

The interpreter translated quickly and Diego nodded.

"Our society cannot function if people do not respect the rights and the property of other people. You have not always been careful to do that." Warren paused, his decision hanging in the air. "Yet I find that in this instance there may have been extenuating circumstances which should be taken into account."

Meredith drew in her breath. She did not dare to hope, yet Warren had said her very own words—*extenuating circumstances*. Could it be that . . .

"Mr. Gutierrez, a judge cannot afford to gamble, because if he makes a mistake, other people can get hurt, innocent people. And so a judge finds himself in the difficult position of having to weigh what is fair to society against what is fair to the individual defendant. A judge must somehow protect the rights of both, and it is very, very hard sometimes to know what to do."

Tension crackled in the air. It was impossible to tell which way Warren would go. It seemed that no one drew breath in the entire courtroom.

Warren sighed softly. "I have decided to put my faith in you and give you a year's probation, where you will be closely supervised." As the interpreter said the words, Diego broke into a smile as bright as a Christmas tree. But the smile faded quickly as Warren continued in a voice edged with harshness. "But you must not let me down. You must honor the terms of your probation and respect the rights and property of other people. Because I promise you, if you appear in this court before me again, charged with another offense, you're going to prison and you'll be an old, old man when you finally get out. I'm warning you, Mr.

Gutierrez, this is your *last chance.* Make the most of it." And suddenly Warren rose. "Court dismissed," he said, as the bailifff called everyone to their feet.

The courtroom became a place of commotion as Diego's family fell upon him, kissing him and congratulating Scott Palmer, his lawyer. Meredith edged into the crowd to remind Diego that he would need to come by her office before going back home. His handshake became a hug, and he whispered in frantic Spanish, *"Gracias, gracias, señorita, muchas gracias."*

Her heart bursting with gratitude that Warren had given consideration to the human factors involved, Meredith hurried back to chambers to thank him. She barely made it past his secretary, who seemed to consider herself a mastiff at the gate to protect the lord and master. But even Miss Tuttle obeyed Warren, and his voice over the intercom said, "Send her in."

Meredith hurried into chambers, eager to leave the disapproving frown of Miss Tuttle behind, joy driving all of the previous night's confusion out of her mind. Her smile was dazzling, and she extended her right hand to shake his. "Thank you, Warren. I'm so grateful to you," she said, feeling a sudden shyness.

His hand barely touched hers and dropped it immediately. His face was cold, his lips set in a hard line. She thought she could see a pallor under his tan. What was wrong? She felt a nervous churning in her stomach.

His voice when he spoke was harsh. "I never allow my personal feelings to interfere with my duty as a judge," he said. "This has nothing to do with what happened last night. After considering all the factors in this situation—"

"Nothing to do with what happened last night? What on earth do you mean?" Meredith interrupted.

"I mean that you don't need to credit your personal

charms with today's victory, Miss Jennings. Believe me, it would take more than a kiss or two to bribe me."

"Bribe you? Is that what you think?" Astonishment washed over Meredith.

"Shouldn't I? You obviously tried to set me up. Really, Miss Jennings, you should have more confidence in your abilities as a probation officer. You're good at your job. You don't have to resort to your physical attractions. Believe me, they didn't affect the outcome of this morning's hearing. My decision was based on the facts, and only on the facts. So don't give yourself the credit. You'd be sadly mistaken."

Warren's words struck Meredith like blows from a hammer. Her face drained of its color, and when she tried to speak in self-defense, she found her throat too tight for words to escape. Tears filling her brown eyes, she turned and bolted from his office without another word. The secretary muttered something but Meredith pushed past, ignoring her, hurrying to the safety of her cubicle at the probation office.

But there was no safety there, either. The news of Diego's suspended sentence had preceded Meredith, and her colleagues drifted by her office to congratulate her. Blundering as always, Harvey managed to say exactly the wrong words when he told Meredith she had really managed "to put this one over." Harvey was absolutely at a loss when Meredith broke into tears, and the more he tried to comfort her, the more she cried. Bewildered, he finally left her alone, though her sobs could be heard through the wall that separated their offices.

Susan Ortega, whose office was next to Meredith's, came in to see if she could help. "What's wrong?" she said sympathetically, patting Meredith's shoulder.

Meredith lifted her tear-stained face. "Judge Baxter was mad and chewed me out."

"In the courtroom?"

"No, in chambers."

"Oh, well, you shouldn't worry about that. One time Judge Berenson got mad at me and reprimanded me in front of the whole courtroom. These judges—you just have to learn how to put up with their egos."

"He didn't have to insult me!"

"I'm sure it was nothing personal. He probably had a bad day and took it out on you. You should be glad he did it in private. When Judge Berenson jumped on me, the whole probation department heard about it. I thought I would never live it down." She grimaced, remembering the old wound.

"Oh, Susan, that must have been awful."

"It was, for a while. Until some new story came along and got everybody's attention."

"Thanks, Susan. You've been a big help."

"It happens to the best of us," Susan said philosophically. "Why don't you run down to the restroom and wash your face? You'll feel better. I'll tell these curiosity-seekers to leave you alone, okay?"

"Thanks again." They walked out the door together, Susan to go back to her office and Meredith to go to the restroom. When Meredith had washed her face and pulled herself together, she realized that Susan had not even asked what Judge Baxter had said. Everybody's life was such an open book in this crowded, busy office that secrets were almost impossible to keep. Meredith felt grateful that Susan had respected her privacy.

She poured herself a cup of coffee and noticed that she was the object of curious glances, but fortunately nobody said anything to her. At some point Diego came by for his instructions, and Meredith found she hardly had the energy to talk to him. It was a relief when he left, because she couldn't bear to be reminded of Warren's accusations, or of his kiss last night.

At noon she made her escape from the office and spent the lunch hour lying on her bed at home staring at the ceiling. She forced herself to repeat every word and every action of the night before and of the morning, searching for a clue to Warren's behavior. How could he think she had used sexual attraction to influence his decision? Her body had responded to his magnetism entirely of its own volition, and Diego had been the furthest thing from her mind. In fact, she had chastised herself for failing to think of Diego, for thinking only of Warren and his nearness, his touch. . . .

Tormented though she was, Meredith had no answer. She rose with a sigh and fixed her makeup, dreading an afternoon of more stares. Sliding her feet into open-toed high heels, Meredith decided to spend the afternoon in the field checking probationers on their jobs. It would get her out of the office, and it needed to be done anyway. She was already two weeks behind with her job-site visits. She called Harvey to tell him she would be out in the field all afternoon but would come by the office before she finished to check the mail.

Meredith was wearing a copper-colored silk print dress that matched her eyes and emphasized the blondness of her hair. She had selected it carefully this morning, knowing Warren would see her and wanting to look her best. She uttered a rueful laugh, thinking that this favorite dress would be in and out of sanitation trucks, hospital washrooms, and service stations where her probationers had jobs. Usually she wore something casual for her job visits, but today her probationers were treated to Meredith at her prettiest. Their sincere compliments warmed her heart, and by afternoon she was feeling much more cheerful. Genuine admiration from males who expected absolutely nothing in return took away some of the sting of Warren's words, though she still felt an urgent need to make him understand that he was wrong. Maybe she would get a chance someday; in the meantime, she would have to be satisfied knowing that she had had no ulterior motives.

Late in the afternoon she went back to the probation office and found a note from Harvey on her desk asking that the order granting Diego's probation be filed in the district clerk's office. She glanced at her watch—4:55. If she hurried, she could get it filed before closing time. She telephoned Jo Betsy, her friend in the clerk's office, and asked her not to close before she got there. Then she hurried back out into the October sunshine, crossed Guadalupe Street, and raced up the stairs to the third floor just as the shade was snapped shut. Jo Betsy, always obliging, quickly filed the court order, passing on the latest news while she worked. "What's the latest on you and Scott?" Jo Betsy wanted to know.

"Scott? Oh, nothing new. We're just friends, that's all."

Jo Betsy's lips formed a sly smile. "That's not the way Scott tells it," she said. "He thinks you're mighty special."

Meredith's face burned. Courthouse gossip seemed to be everybody's favorite game, and being seen with the same man twice in a row was enough to set tongues wagging. She did her best to steer Jo Betsy's thinking in a new direction, though without much success.

The elevator door whooshed shut just as Meredith stepped out of the clerk's office, and she quickly pressed the button to see if the door would open again. It was hot and she felt too tired to use the stairs. The elevator doors slid open again, and to Meredith's surprise, revealed Warren as the passenger whose trip down had been halted by her action. Flustered, she stood there, not sure whether to get inside or wait for the next elevator.

"Are you going to get in or not?" he inquired. His tone was as cool as it had been that morning in his office. Frustration rose in Meredith. What right did he have to misjudge her so? She stepped inside the elevator and they made the short ride down in silence, each suffocatingly aware of the other's presence. Meredith stepped out onto the marble courthouse floor while Warren held the door for her. Quickly making up her mind, she turned and gave him a pleading look.

"Warren, please, you misunderstood what happened last night. I can explain—" she stammered.

"Can you now? How interesting." He seemed not to care and started toward the side door.

"Damn it, Warren, I want you to listen to me."

He turned to face her, the haughty look on his face relaxing slightly. "Are you going to stand here and screech at me like a fishwife for all the world to hear?" he asked.

"If that's what it takes to get you to listen, yes." Meredith was angry again. There was something about Warren that brought out the extremes in her emotions. At the moment she couldn't care less about the other people crowding the hall.

"This is really not the place for a private discussion, Meredith," Warren said as he steered her out the door and across the street to Wooldridge Park. "Do you really want a public brawl?" he asked when they came to a stop under the oak and pecan trees. "Then have at it. If you aren't going to worry about your career, I'm not going to worry about mine."

Meredith, abashed, looked around, for the first time

aware of their surroundings. Clusters of workers were leaving the courthouse and the annex building, headed for their cars in the parking garage. Curious glances shot their way, and Meredith knew it would be all over the office by Monday morning that she and Judge Baxter had had an argument in front of the courthouse on Friday afternoon. "You're right. This isn't the time or place. I'm sorry."

"Do you have a better suggestion?" he asked. Her apology had softened him a little.

She thought for a minute. "If you don't have to be somewhere else, maybe we could have a drink."

Warren looked at his watch, his eyes thoughtful.

"Never mind," Meredith said, thinking better of her suggestion. "I know it's Friday night and I'm sure you have other plans."

"And no doubt you do, too," he countered.

"Not until later."

"How much later?"

"About nine."

"This is as good a time as any, I suppose." He reflected a moment more. "Tell you what, let's go by my apartment so I can make a phone call, then I'll be free until nine o'clock, too."

Warren's "apartment" turned out to be a luxury condominium at Cambridge Towers a few short blocks away. In a building favored by prominent state politicians, it fairly reeked of exclusivity. A doorman in the cavernous lobby greeted them and ushered them onto the elevator. They rode to the top floor, where Warren enjoyed a tastefully decorated penthouse apartment. The elegance was suited to Warren's station in life, yet at the same time it had an earthiness that no decorator had provided. A pecan wood armoire in the living room had been converted to a bar, and Warren offered Meredith a drink. She decided on a wine cooler, and Warren fixed Scotch and water for himself. Sipping it slowly, he excused himself to make his telephone call. Left alone in the room, Meredith looked around at the interesting combination of wood, leather, and brass. A Chinese vase and screen added delicacy to the setting. Meredith thought of her own snug home with its polished wood floors, braided rug, and maple rocking chair, and knew she and Warren were certainly not in the same league. She leaned back into the corner of the low-slung sofa, flipping pages of the current *Smithsonian* magazine on the black enameled coffee table. Well, at least it wasn't the *American Bar Journal,* she thought with a wry grin.

She sipped the wine and tried to organize her thoughts before Warren returned. At the office it had seemed imperative that she convince Warren she had no ulterior motives for her behavior with him last night. Her passionate response had surprised her as much as it had him, and she was frankly a little embarrassed about it. How could she have been so abandoned with a *judge?* It was reckless and stupid and it undermined her role as a professional. Contrary to Warren's belief, it had absolutely nothing to do with her probationer; it was a response to Warren himself. Here in his apartment, though, the world of work seemed far away, and it was going to be awkward to deal with the issue. She sat up straight-backed on the sofa, dreading another confrontation.

Warren paused in the doorway and took note of her rigid posture. She must be getting ready for another battle, he thought with dismay. At least, whatever she said to him here wouldn't be fodder for the gossip-mill. He had met her only yesterday and already the courthouse was buzzing. His position required absolute discretion, and he did not enjoy being the subject of that kind of gossip. He had to run for re-election every four years, and even idle talk without any substance behind it could be damaging. By Monday their argument on the courthouse lawn would be common knowledge.

Warren was angry with Meredith, and angry with himself for not being able to control his feelings when he was with her. There had been women in his life, but never one who could get under his skin the way Meredith had. Self-discipline was his stock-in-trade. He prided himself on being a reasonable man, but with her, reason gave way to passion. He glanced again at her erect figure on the couch and glared. Damn, damn! He wanted to get this over with.

He walked across the plush carpet and sat down on a black enameled chair across from Meredith. "Could I get you some more wine?" he asked politely. He was determined to maintain absolute control of himself.

"No, this is fine, thanks," she answered, lifting her head. For a moment their eyes met and neither could think of anything to say. The tension level rose with the silence. Warren sipped his drink and waited. She had requested this meeting, and she would have to make the first move.

Meredith nervously cleared her throat. "It's a little hard to know where to start," she said at last.

Warren sipped his drink. He was still annoyed enough to be reluctant to make it easy for her. Let her squirm for a while.

His silence nettled her and provided just the impetus she needed. Sparks flashed in her brown eyes, and her voice was rich with injured innocence when she spoke.

"I'm sure you realize that this is embarrassing for me," she said. "I made a fool of myself last night. I took myself too seriously, I took Diego too seriously, and I . . . took *you* too seriously." A pink stain crept up her cheeks. "No matter how it seems to you, I didn't—Diego wasn't the reason I—you were so—" She broke off in confusion. "And then when you thought it was because . . . You were angry with me for . . ." She twisted her hands together and peeked in his direction. He was grinning! Her incoherent explanation had overcome his determination to stay cool. She was just too endearing—and amusing.

"Damn you, Warren Baxter!" She picked up a silk tapestry pillow from the sofa and tossed it at him.

He caught it neatly in one hand. "Are you trying to tell me that when you kissed me last night, Diego was the farthest thing from your mind?" he asked, his grin getting wider. "Really, Meredith, I'm flattered. To think I gave the credit to Diego when it was *me* all the time!"

They both broke into laughter and the tension was gone. Meredith stood to leave. "Thank goodness this is settled," she said with a sigh of relief. "I've been upset all day worrying about it."

"You don't have to be in any hurry," Warren said. "It's still early. Would you like something to eat? I can rustle up some cheese and crackers."

Meredith realized that she had eaten nothing all day, and feeling famished, she accepted the offer of food. She followed Warren into an immaculate kitchen and peeked over his head into an almost-empty refrigerator. "Do you live on cheese and crackers?" she asked in surprise.

"I never eat here. There's never any time to cook."

"Don't you get tired of eating out?"

"Sure I do. But I have too many social obligations to do anything else." He piled cubes of cheese and stacks of crackers and chips on a crystal platter. "Here—this is the best I can do." He was matter-of-fact, just an ordinary bachelor with an empty cupboard, and Meredith realized that he was being himself, for once not playing the role of judge. She began to relax.

They went back into the living room and sat down at opposite ends of the couch. Warren had taken off his jacket and tie while he was on the telephone, and Meredith leaned back, comfortable now in the soft pillows.

"I envy you this couch," she murmured. "Mine is as hard as a board. Nobody ever wants to sit on it." She unconsciously wiggled her toes. "This is heavenly."

Warren reached out with his foot and playfully nudged her toes. "Sometimes you're like a little kid," he said, a smile in his eyes. "I bet your feet hurt with those silly shoes you have on."

"Oh, they do." She laughed at the three-inch heels on her shoes. "That's female vanity for you, teetering around on heels like that."

Warren lifted her feet into his lap and removed her shoes, tossing them over by the coffee table. He massaged first her arches and then her ankles. Meredith ignored the warning buzzer in her brain and snuggled into her corner of the couch, knowing she was being reckless but tempted by the feel of his strong fingers. "Mmmm," she sighed.

"Like that?" Of course she did. He could tell. "Turn this way and I'll do your neck." Meredith obeyed without stopping to think. She moved to the opposite end of the couch, reversing her body, her back next to

Warren. His hands lifted the blonde hair from the nape of her neck and gently massaged the tension from her back and shoulders. The warmth from his body coursed through hers, and a delicious lethargy washed over her. She snuggled against his chest, completely relaxed.

"That's enough. I don't want to spoil you," he said. There was a sort of gruffness in his voice that had not been there before. His fingers drifted across her shoulder and dropped.

Meredith turned to speak, but not a word left her lips. Because when she turned, their eyes met. Warren swept her into his arms and buried his lips in the tender nape of her neck. Her body, which had been so languid a moment before, now pulsated with desire. She lifted his head from the delicious hollow of her neck, her mouth searching for his. Their lips met, parted. She could taste the Scotch on his tongue, and her tongue quivered in response. His hands moved up her body, searching for the soft female warmth of her. His mouth continued to probe hers while his fingers worked with the buttons on her dress. Meredith's arms moved upward, pulled his head back into the hollow of her throat. She could feel his breath hot against her neck, and as his fingers succeeded with the buttons, freeing her breasts, his teeth found their way to her ear and nibbled. Her body ached with wanting.

"Beautiful—you're beautiful," he whispered, his voice husky with desire. "Your skin is so creamy and soft." He held her body a little apart from him so he could see her better, and when their eyes met, she could see that his had turned smoky, his pupils dilated from passion. She leaned against the hardened strength of his body, wanting to be closer, closer to him. His mouth trailed up her neck, found her warm mouth waiting, longing. He drew her nectar, intoxicated with the sweetness of her.

Warren chuckled against her hair.

"What's so funny?" she asked, her voice tremulous.

"I'm glad I let Diego off, if this is the way you're going to express your gratitude."

"Warren," she whispered. "That's not true."

"No? You could have fooled me." His hands slipped around her, drawing her back closer to his chest. She sat up against him, tension tightening her body.

"Warren, please don't think that."

"It doesn't matter," he murmured, still seeking her mouth with his. "Happens all the time."

Meredith went rigid. Her desire vanished instantly. She pushed Warren away and sat up, blinking her eyes to focus them. She looked down at her disheveled clothing and was embarrassed. Though he reached to pull her back to him, she stood and turned her back, rearranging and buttoning her dress.

"What do you think you're doing?" he asked, angered.

"I'm leaving," she cried, sliding her feet back into her shoes.

"What kind of game are you playing, anyway?"

"I'm not playing any kind of game, can't you understand that?"

"Listen, Meredith. You're no schoolgirl. You knew what you were doing when you came up here."

"I came up here so you could use the telephone," she answered, her voice dull.

"Sure. And let me put my hands all over you. And *enjoyed* it, I might add." Now he stood, towering over her, his voice simmering with frustration.

"Yes. I enjoyed it. But it won't work, Warren."

"You wanted me. Admit it."

Meredith lowered her eyes. "Yes, I did," she whispered. "But you think it was for the wrong reasons."

"It doesn't matter what the reasons are. I told you, it happens all the time."

"To you?"

"No, not to me. But it happens. Trade-offs are just part of the business world. It's the way things are. Diego got his chance, you're glad about that. It gives you a nice, warm feeling about me—so what? Let's just enjoy it." He reached for her again but she evaded him.

"Sorry, I'm just not that grateful," she said, her voice icy. "I guess you think I act this way every time someone does me a favor."

His look was cynical. "Well, you must admit you can come on pretty strong."

She was furious. "You are absolutely despicable! I felt something special, and you've ruined it!"

"It isn't ruined," he said, trying to mollify her. "Or it doesn't have to be. We can keep our personal and professional lives separate. All it takes is for you to forget that you're a probation officer and I'm a judge." He reached for her again, but it was too late. She had had enough.

"We can't just put things into tight little compartments. Life won't let us. I'm leaving, Warren."

"I'll call you a taxi."

"Never mind. I'll walk."

"I told you chivalry and business don't mix. Suit yourself." Warren was absolutely livid with fury and frustrated desire. He was determined to have the last word. "I've had it with schoolgirls. From now on, I want women who know how to separate business and pleasure." Meredith ran from the apartment, but not in time to escape hearing his last words: "Give me a woman like Bettis Langley any day."

Stung to the quick and furious, Meredith turned and shouted, "Go ahead. I'm sure she can turn her feelings on and off the same way *you* do. I'm not that shallow! Goodbye, Warren."

Chapter Three

Meredith peered into her bathroom mirror, applying the last of a heavy layer of iridescent eye shadow to her eyelids. Thick mascara had turned her long eyelashes to a black fringe. Her slim forefinger daubed extra blusher onto her high cheekbones. She stood back from the mirror, taking another critical look at her reflection, then reached for the flowing dark wig she had rented at the theatrical costume shop and gently nudged it onto her head. She certainly hoped nobody would recognize her in this outfit.

It had been Scott Palmer's idea. Halloween was one of the most festive nights in Austin. Not only a night for small children to trick or treat, but also a night when adults threw themselves wholeheartedly into the revelry of masquerade. Scott had gone with Meredith to the costume shop and selected the belly dancer outfit, with gauzy skirts and sequined bra-top. At the time, Meredith had been so depressed over the fiasco in Warren's apartment that she would have agreed to almost any suggestion that would save her from having to make a decision. But now that she stood here in the skimpy, revealing outfit, she felt definitely uneasy. Her own sensual response to Warren had stirred up feelings within her that she had never experienced before, and to view herself in alluring bareness reminded her too painfully of her wanton surrender to those feelings. Brazen hussy, she scolded, scowling at her reflection.

A knock at the door announced Scott's arrival, and he was so enthusiastic about Meredith's transformation that he brushed away all her fears. Scott had turned his creative genius to developing the perfect costume for himself and was wearing the rubber face mask of an elderly man, complete with flowing silver hair. He had borrowed a pair of green pajamas and a plastic name bracelet from the hospital, and a rented wheelchair was folded and waiting in his car. He was absolutely delighted, both with himself and with Meredith.

"This is great, Meredith. Nobody else's costumes will even come close to ours."

"It worries me, Scott. What if somebody recognizes us?"

"Don't be silly. Put your veil on, and with all that makeup, and the wig, nobody will ever guess." As far as Scott was concerned, the most important part of the festivity was being so perfectly disguised that no one would ever recognize them. He was an old pro at dressing for Halloween, a habit he had gotten into during his law school days when the U.T. Law School was the scene for the biggest party of the year—the "Fall Drunk," held each Halloween. He was proud to boast that he had not only won the prize for best costume for three years running, but he had also been named the "Fall Drunk" for each of his three years in law school—which was to say that he was the drunkest person at the party. And, laughing at his own pun, he reminded Meredith that to be the drunkest person at a law school party was to beat out some very "stiff" competition.

Something about being in costume released their inhibitions, and by the time they had driven to Sixth Street, where all the clubs were having parties, both Meredith and Scott were as exhilarated as children on the last day of school. Crowds of people lined Sixth Street, and they joined them, moving from club to club, the throngs shouting to be heard over the blaring of the bands. Meredith walked behind Scott, pushing him in the wheelchair, and from time to time he would stop to take a swig of beer. The festive spirit was contagious, and soon Meredith found herself wiggling her hips as she pushed Scott in the wheelchair. Their costumes were the hit of the evening, and every place they went on the busy street, people turned and laughed.

After they had "done" Sixth Street, Scott decided he wanted to go to Fiesta Gardens for the law school party, and try to recapture his past glories by winning the "Fall Drunk" award again. Meredith suspected they did not belong there, but Scott convinced her that Halloween was a time for revelry and daring. Cloudy skies hid the stars as they walked back to Scott's car, and Meredith was glad the weather had stayed warm or otherwise she would have frozen in her skimpy costume. She was having a wonderful time wandering around and looking at the people. Scott was amusing company and the evening was a delightful entertainment. Meredith decided that never again would she sit home on Halloween and miss all this fun.

It wasn't far to Fiesta Gardens, but Scott's driving was beginning to show the effects of his drinking, and he missed two turns before getting to the right place. The law school crowd was still going strong, and after looking around at all the clever costumes—everything from a classic Dracula to elaborate political jokes or costumes depicting the latest fad—Meredith realized it was his prior law school parties that made Scott put such store on originality. He bought their tickets, and Meredith wheeled him to the beer kegs set up under a post-oak tree where he immediately began to toss down one plastic cupful of beer after another. Fortunately, he was seated in the wheelchair; otherwise he would soon have been staggering.

A commotion nearby signaled the arrival of the press. A TV camera crew with floodlights on a portable camera started through the park to take pictures of the most interesting costumes. The floodlights landed on Meredith and Scott, and Meredith noticed the cameraman's assistant scrambling off in the darkness.

In a moment he returned, Bettis Langley in tow. Bettis was dressed as a gypsy in an off-the-shoulder peasant blouse that emphasized her tanned good looks. Behind her Meredith was surprised to see Warren Baxter, looking for all the world like he had just gotten down off a horse, so perfectly at ease was he in a Western-cut shirt and skintight faded Levi's, a cowboy hat tilted rakishly atop his dark hair, and one arm draped casually across Bettis's shoulder.

Bettis the newswoman came alive. Delighted at the interesting tableau offered by a belly dancer attending to a wizened old man in a wheelchair, she approached Meredith and Scott with a bright smile, the camera aimed at them. Meredith felt a fleeting anxiety that she would be recognized and reached to be sure her veil and wig were still intact. She stole a glance at Warren, standing just outside the circle of floodlights, and noticed that his eyes were raking her exposed flesh. She tossed her head in a gesture of defiance. Let him look! He couldn't possibly recognize her.

Scott was delighting the audience with his droll imitation of an octogenarian. When Bettis Langley inquired the reason for his long life, he promptly cackled, "Booze, women and dissipated living." She then turned the microphone to Meredith and asked for an impromptu belly dance. Meredith recoiled in horror, but the request was quickly echoed by the horde of men who surrounded the circle of light. She shook her head in confusion, and when they continued to whistle and cheer, she blushed in embarrassment. Bettis continued to urge, sensing that a provocative dance would be an effective addition to the news spot.

Meredith turned aside and her glance caught Warren's and locked. His eyes narrowed and he nodded imperceptibly, then beckoned to her with a $100 bill. "Just a short dance?" he taunted.

The crowd went wild. "Dance! Dance!" they demanded.

Whether it was the wine she had drunk, Warren's presence, the boisterous crowd, or the disguise that made her lose her inhibitions, Meredith never knew. But when Bettis prompted her again, she felt a wild, unfettered excitement well up in her and she threw her body into a tantalizing, rhythmic belly dance.

Around them people gathered to cheer her on, and Meredith circled the group, arms waving gracefully above her head, hips rolling. She leaned against Scott briefly with a soft smile, and he reached inside his pocket for a dollar bill, which he stuck inside the band of her skirt as her hips swayed near enough. The crowd applauded, and then all the men were reaching in their pockets, urging Meredith to dance nearer, that they too might put the bills in her skirt band or bra-top. Her smile became a wicked gleam, and she enticed them, hips moving faster and faster to their clapping hands, feet moving in graceful rhythm to an inner music that only she could hear. Head flung back, eyes narrowed to slits, she circled the group again, this time edging closer and closer to Warren. A muscle tensed in his jaw; his nostrils flared. Passion swept through both of them with the force of a rocket launch.

Meredith's breasts brushed his arm, her hips swayed nearer, then away. Taut with desire, he beckoned with the folded bill. Pulse racing, she danced back in his direction, tantalizingly near. She reached out with a willowy movement of her hand, but he shook his head, daring her to brave the sexual currents that raged between them. She leaned her torso toward him and threw back her head, circling him, her body swaying nearly backward, castanets clicking at her sides. He loomed above her, eyes blazing, shutting out the rest of the world, and she danced, dancing only for him. Against the midnight sky she could see nothing but the fires of passion that glowed in his eyes.

From somewhere she could hear Bettis's voice talking to the television audience and Meredith drifted back to the real world. Slowly she drew her body upright again, swaying back against Warren one last time. His fingers reached out quickly and pushed the bill against her breast. Underneath the gauze veil her lips parted in a sensual, mysterious smile, showing her gleaming white teeth. Then, in a triumphant finish, she leapt upward, falling forward in a graceful bow. The crowd around her cheered and whistled, stomping their feet and shouting appreciatively. She felt Scott take her hand and squeeze it.

"Nobody would ever have guessed there was a red-hot firecracker wrapped up inside that demure little probation officer," he whispered. "Where have you been hiding, anyway?" Meredith laughed, enjoying his confusion, but she quickly became her old self again. That uninhibited slave-girl was for Warren alone—and then only when she was in disguise.

To Scott's great disappointment, he was disqualified from entering the "Fall Drunk" contest because he was a post-graduate—although the judges conceded that he would easily have won if he had been eligible. He was far and away the drunkest person at the party. After the awards were announced, the party began to break up, no doubt to reassemble in smaller groups at other places, and Meredith was left with the problem of getting Scott home. She had no trouble rolling him in the wheelchair to his car, but once there, he stubbornly insisted on driving. She coaxed and wheedled, but to no avail. Drive he would, no matter how much she objected. Meredith estimated the number of blocks to her house and decided maybe Scott could make it that far, if she was alert to grab the wheel. Once they reached her house, she figured she could get him inside and sober him up with strong, hot coffee. It was the best she could do under the circumstances; she certainly didn't want to spend the night in the park.

Unfortunately, Scott was drunker than Meredith thought. His desire to recapture his hard-drinking student days had clouded his judgment and before the car had gone a block it was almost out of control.

Meredith frantically pleaded with Scott to pull over and let her take the wheel, but he pushed her away. "Leave me alone," he said, his voice slurred. "I can drive." The signal light at the corner flashed red, and Scott threw on the brakes, squealing to a sudden stop that stalled the engine. He ground the key in the ignition, but it didn't catch. Behind them a car had stopped, and the driver got out and started toward Scott's car. In the rearview mirror Scott could see the slim figure in cowboy clothes illuminated by the streetlight above.

"Oh, my God. It's Judge Baxter," he said, anguished. "Oh, my God, he'll take away my law license. Oh, my God." Before Meredith could turn around, knuckles rapped against the side window, and Scott rolled down the glass.

"Yes, sir?" he asked, his voice the whimper of a naughty puppy.

"What do you think you're doing? I followed you down the street and you were weaving from one side to the other. Don't you know that's unsafe?" Warren's voice was stern and cold.

Scott looked down at his hospital pajamas. In his drunken state, desperation drove him to fabricate. "I'm sick," he said, weakly, and rolled his head back against the car seat. "Help me." Meredith put her hand over her mouth to smother a laugh. Poor Scott. But she kept her head averted and dared not say a word. So far they hadn't been identified, but if Warren recognized her voice, their secret would be out. And that dance! He mustn't ever find out that it was Meredith who danced that shameless dance for him!

"You, miss," Warren barked. "Get out so I can move him into your seat." Meredith got out on the passenger side and kept a safe distance while Warren shoved Scott, none too gently, into the other seat. Scott moaned, feigning sickness, which panic had now made almost legitimate.

"Where do you live?" Warren asked.

Scott moaned and leaned his masked face away from Warren, his words blurred.

Disgusted, Warren turned to Meredith. "All right. You drive my car and I'll follow you."

Meredith stared bleakly at the silver Mercedes. She didn't know whether she could drive it.

"Do what I said!" Warren insisted. "You won't have any trouble driving my car. And obviously you can't manage this man or you wouldn't be in the car with him."

Meredith didn't dare argue for fear she would reveal her identity. She hurried back to Warren's car and luckily had no problem putting it in gear and pulling into the street while Warren took the wheel of Scott's car. She led Warren sedately down the back streets to Scott's condominium on Riverside Drive. By the time they arrived, Scott had fallen asleep and couldn't be awakened. Warren dragged him out of the car, his arms around his chest, and directed Meredith to carry Scott's feet. Somehow they got him up the stairs, and Warren unceremoniously dumped him onto the bed and tossed his car keys onto the dresser.

"What about you?" Warren asked. "Are you staying the night with him?"

She looked up in surprise and shook her head. "I'll . . . take a taxi," she stammered, trying to disguise her voice.

"At 2:00 A.M.—in that getup? Who do you think you're kidding?"

Meredith nervously stroked the black hair of the wig. Her body was sweaty from the exertion of dragging Scott up the stairs, and her makeup was beginning to smear. She glanced in the mirror and saw that she looked a fright. She'd probably be picked up for prostitution if she appeared on the street alone.

Warren reached for the doorknob and turned the lock. "Go get in my car and I'll take you home. It's the least I can do after that dance you gave me."

Meredith reached for the bill he had wedged against her breast, her face flaming with embarrassment, and tried to force it into his hand. "No," she whispered.

"Don't keep arguing," he answered impatiently, refusing the bill. "You're the most stubborn woman I've ever met. Do what I said."

It was useless to argue. And Meredith was terrified of revealing her identity. She ran lightly down the steps and climbed into the Mercedes.

"Where do you live?" Warren asked, climbing in beside her.

"Hyde Park. Just off Duval."

They rode in an uncomfortable silence. Warren was preoccupied, and Meredith thought the ride could not end soon enough. Being alone in the car with him with so much of her flesh exposed and Warren's body straining against skintight cowboy clothes created the same kind of sexual tension that had precipitated her dance. Forgotten for the moment were their constant misunderstandings, and Meredith was aware of Warren only as a desirable male. She turned and stared blankly out the window, trying to control her thoughts.

When Warren broke the silence, his voice was angry. "How could you be so stupid as to get into a car with someone that drunk?" he said. "Don't you know you could have gotten yourself or someone else killed? That guy was weaving all over the street." His words poured out in a tirade of angry recriminations. Meredith had no way to defend herself because she knew she had been foolish, but it hurt her pride for Warren to tell her so. His denunciations grew more scathing, and she flinched under his words. But she dared not speak or he would recognize her voice. And if he knew that it was Scott and Meredith who were weaving down the street, officers of his court . . . no, he mustn't ever find out. She drew herself into the corner and concentrated on the passing streets.

They pulled into her darkened driveway and she jumped out of the car, Warren close behind her. "I'll see you to your door," he said. "After all the trouble to get you home safely, I wouldn't want somebody to grab you here."

"Sorry for your trouble," Meredith said, sniffing. She needed a tissue. She was afraid she was going to cry. She fitted her housekey into the lock.

"Let me turn on the lights to be sure it's safe," Warren said, his voice still imperious. He followed her through the door and snapped on the lamp in the living room, then walked through the house, turning on lights. The little house looked cheerful and safe. Meredith was glad to be home.

"Everything seems fine," Warren said.

"Thank you," she answered, averting her head.

"Sure you don't need help with anything else?" he asked. There was something taunting in his voice. What did he mean? Meredith did not realize that the soft lamplight bathed her skin in silken beauty and that the heavy makeup on her eyes gave them a sensual, mysterious shimmer. Her lips trembled beneath the gauze veil.

"It's a shame for such a beautiful woman to be cheated out of her lover's goodnight kiss," Warren murmured, his voice thick. He reached over and turned off the light, then pulled Meredith into his arms. His fingers lifted her veil, and his lips met hers in a searching kiss that left her breathless and longing for more. Again his mouth closed against hers, tasting the sweetness, touching, probing, gently caressing, heart pounding against heart. His arms drew her closer and closer, until she was lost in his strength. His lips traveled down her bare shoulders, gently kissing her tingling skin, darting nearer and nearer the electric pulsing of her breasts. Each time his lips lingered, then teased and moved away. She moaned softly and drew his head back up, his mouth to hers, warm now with wanting, ecstasy in her tongue, her lips. His strong arms pulled her hips against his, hands cupped against her so that she could feel the excitement surge in him. His mouth plunged downward, seeking, searching, finding. Meredith trembled in his arms, aching with desire, everything forgotten but this man who thrilled her beyond belief. He could feel her yield against him and knew that she was his for the taking. His mouth traveled back up to hers, tasted again its delicious sweetness that begged for more of him. His hands cupped her face, gently kissed her eyelids, and ended with a light peck on her nose that broke the spell.

"I don't want to take advantage of you," he murmured, his voice struggling to regain control. "I came in with you to be sure you were safe." He dropped a quick kiss on her lips that promised nothing and withheld everything. Meredith protested with a soft moan and put her arms back around his neck.

"Please don't go," she whispered. She could not bear for him to leave. Her desire for him was overpowering. She lifted her face for another kiss.

Biting his lip, Warren fought for self-control. He had to resist her, though everything inside him clamored for release. If he stayed, she would regret it and be embarrassed in the morning. He clasped her upper arms and firmly moved her away from him. "Not tonight," he answered. "Some other time, when you've had time to think about it." His eyes danced with amusement, but in the dark Meredith could not see it. He reached out and flipped on the light again. Hurriedly Meredith pulled the veil back over her face, but nothing could hide her pupils, dilated with desire. Things were happening too fast. Her response to Warren's sexuality was so immediate, so complete, that when he pulled away it was like being on a runaway rollercoaster with her emotions continuing to hurtle off the track.

She leaned against the door, her body shaking, unable to think or respond to the change in him. "But, why—" she asked in dismay.

"Because it's not a good idea to get involved with strangers." He stepped out the door and onto the porch.

Meredith wanted to throw herself into his arms and tell him they were not strangers, but his parting words stopped her. "Besides, I have to go. I'm late as it is." Meredith slammed the door behind him and gave herself up to murderous thoughts of Bettis Langley.

Chapter Four

Meredith dialed another telephone number, her eye on the clock. Ten minutes to seven. This would have to be her last call. She glanced around the room where campaign volunteers were all dialing in frantic haste.

"Hello . . . Mrs. Waters?" Meredith inquired. "I'm calling for 'Rocky' Rockwell to remind you to vote. Have you been to the polls yet? . . . It's very important, Mrs. Waters. Can you make it over to your precinct before the polls close? I encourage you to vote for Rocky. Please, hurry, before the polls close. Thank you."

Meredith broke the connection and dropped the

phone into the cradle. Her shoulders ached and her throat was raw. She had come to campaign headquarters immediately after work every night for the past week, making literally hundreds of telephone calls. She had been glad to stay busy, too busy to think . . . almost. Yet even with dozens of calls to make each night, her mind would sometimes sneak out of control and think forbidden thoughts of Warren Baxter. Meredith's confusion had grown with each passing day. She knew she had made a fool of herself with that torrid dance on Halloween night. Why had she given in to a crazy impulse that way? And then at the door, when Warren had kissed her goodnight . . . She had to be honest with herself, she had practically tried to seduce the man. Her body had demanded fulfillment, yearned for him to possess her—like some harlot, she thought, remembering with flaming cheeks the way her body had molded itself to his. And then to be rejected! How humiliating! Thank heavens Warren did not know her identity. He must never know, *never*.

Yet the mere thought of Warren made Meredith tingle with excitement. Her stomach tightened at the memory of his mouth searing hers. Each time Meredith's thoughts would go this far but no farther, as her mind came to a screeching halt with the memory of Warren's final words, "I have to go. I'm late as it is." Then anger would drive away desire and leave her shaking. Bettis Langley! How could Warren kiss her that way and then leave her—mid-kiss—for another woman? Meredith remembered the way her body had shaken with frustrated desire and rage when Warren had left her standing at her door. He had been so damned jaunty when he left, too, almost as if he had been laughing at her. It must be the way he amused himself, using his animal magnetism to make a woman wild with wanting, then leaving her in empty confusion. Meredith shook her head and made herself stop these tormenting thoughts. She was dangerously near tears, and she must control herself in front of all these other campaign workers.

"All right, everybody," cried Vivian Thompson, the director of volunteers. "That does it. The polls are closed now, and there's nothing more for us to do but wait for the votes to be counted. Thank you all for your hard work, and let's just hope it pays off with a victory. This state needs Rocky Rockwell."

Vivian was interrupted with cheers from the crowd. Then she added, "Rocky is expecting everybody at victory headquarters, so go on down to the Driskill Hotel. There will be food and drinks—"

More applause from the workers. They were probably more hungry than excited at this stage of the campaign. ". . . and I'm sure the television stations will be there with cameras—just a reminder, in case some of you want to freshen up before you see yourselves on TV." Vivian was amiable and jolly, ideal for her role. She had generated enough enthusiasm to win World War III, and if Rocky won, it would be because her volunteers had done the impossible. She had insisted that Rocky reward them properly, with excellent food, drinks and public thanks. Vivian gave a last, resounding hurrah and slumped into a chair, grateful that there wouldn't be another campaign for four more years.

"Can I give you a ride to the Driskill, Vivian?" Meredith asked. "You look exhausted."

"Oh, honey, you bet your sweet life. And see if you can get somebody to carry me to the car, will you? I swear I can't move another step." Vivian's hearty laugh shook her entire body.

* * *

The upstairs ballroom of the Driskill Hotel was packed with well-wishers and supporters. Meredith inched her way through the crowd toward the buffet table heaped high with sandwiches and snacks. Heavens! thought Meredith, this is election night pandemonium. This was her first campaign experience, and she had to admit that even though she had fought a battle with the blues over Warren Baxter, the campaign itself had been a lark. She had loved talking to the voters, handing out brochures and explaining why Rocky would make a great governor. The telephone calls had gotten tedious after the first hundred or so, but even after that she had felt that she was making an important contribution—one that could easily make a difference in the outcome of the gubernatorial race. Meredith finally reached the table and helped herself to a hearty ham sandwich, then started the more difficult struggle toward the bar. It seemed that there were more thirsty workers than hungry ones, and Meredith munched her sandwich for an interminable period of time waiting her turn for a drink.

"Better take two while you have a chance," muttered an impatient voice at her elbow.

Meredith turned and found herself staring into the face of her boss, Harvey Gilstrap, whose cherubic features were glistening as a result of struggling to make his way through the crowd. "Why, Harvey, what are you doing here? I didn't know you were working for the Rockwell campaign."

"Now, Meredith," he answered, his eyes twinkling, "you know I delegate work better than I do it." She smiled in agreement. Delegation was the secret of Harvey's success—and he did it in a way that brought out the best in his subordinates, because he was not only willing to give them responsibility, he then respected their judgment. He was probably one of the most popular supervisors in Travis County.

Harvey cleared his throat. "Just came down to pay my respects. If Rocky is elected, it will mean some changes for our department, you know."

"Yes, I'm excited about his ideas for penal reform. Drastic measures need to be taken for the State." As usual, when the conversation turned to Meredith's favorite topic, her voice rose with enthusiasm and her cheeks flushed a rosy pink. She spoke breathlessly for several minutes while Harvey nodded his head and tried to figure out how to ease out of the conversation without losing his turn at the bar. If Harvey was restless, however, having heard Meredith on this subject almost daily during the election campaign, someone else was genuinely interested. A gentle hand reached around Harvey's girth and tapped Meredith's shoulder.

"I didn't mean to eavesdrop," interrupted Bettis Langley, "but with so many people crowded together, it's impossible not to overhear."

"Think nothing of it," responded Harvey with heartfelt relief.

"It wasn't a personal conversation at all," Meredith said, trying to be cordial even though her heart sank in dismay at the sight of Bettis Langley in a crisp red suit which accentuated her dark hair. What right did one woman have to look so gorgeous? Meredith's eyes took in the navy and white silk scarf fastened at Bettis's neck with a small gold pin in the shape of a flag. It was an election-night costume that would photograph perfectly for television.

"Haven't I met you somewhere before?" mused Bettis. "You seem vaguely familiar."

Meredith remembered her flamboyant belly dance for television on Halloween night. "I believe I've seen you around the courthouse," she answered, evading the issue. She explained her job as probation officer and was surprised to find that Bettis listened intently to everything she said. Bettis listened not only with her ears, but with her eyes. Her whole body seemed poised, ready to coax if need be to get Meredith to respond. Meredith put aside her animosity and talked, completely relaxed, eager to share her thoughts about rehabilitation of prisoners through a penal system which aimed for something more than punishment. Meredith did not notice when Bettis gave the casual hand signal which elicited a camera crew within seconds; she did not notice the floodlights a few feet away; all she realized was that she had found a sympathetic listener, and Meredith poured out her heart, sharing her concern for the unfortunates who had brushes with the law which so often ruined their lives. Meredith also mentioned her hopes that Rocky Rockwell would be elected so that he could implement a plan that would rescue some of these lives and relieve the burden on society. Meredith never knew that her brown eyes were the focus of a television close-up or that her sincere concern was enough to melt the heart of the most rabid jailer.

"How do you think Rocky will be able to change our state penal system?" Bettis asked, leaning forward.

"It's a difficult task, but I hope he'll take a whole new approach. For instance, why couldn't criminal defendants pay their debt to society in some more constructive way than being locked up in prison? That just costs the state money and returns nothing to the public good.

But if those defendants could actually perform some kind of service, they would feel that they were helping society—and they would be learning job skills that would help them live better lives when their time is up."

"Well, Miss Jennings, it's too bad we don't have more state employees like you who are visionary about their work and not afraid to dream big dreams. Thank you for sharing your thoughts with our television audience." Bettis turned to the camera. "We're going to take a station break and be back in sixty seconds with more news from Rockwell campaign headquarters at the Driskill Hotel. Stay tuned."

Meredith looked at Bettis in shock. "Don't tell me you were filming that conversation!" she wailed.

"You were perfect," Bettis said, smiling. "The folks at home were eating that up. You did more for your cause than the state legislature could do in ten years." Bettis gathered up her things and hurried away to look for another "story," leaving Meredith surprised to find herself the center of an animated group of admirers.

She had been so engrossed in her discussion with Bettis Langley that she had not noticed the TV interview had drawn a crowd of onlookers. Instant celebrity, that's what I am, she thought, enjoying the unsought attention, yet knowing that it would fade as rapidly as it had appeared. Even Harvey Gilstrap, her boss, had become a fascinated listener. His way of congratulating her was to give her a big hug just as Scott Palmer arrived on the scene.

"Hey, Harvey, what's going on?" Scott asked, extricating Meredith from Harvey's grasp.

"Huh?" Harvey twisted his head at the sound of his name.

"You old married lecher, let go of this woman. She belongs to me tonight," Scott said with a grin. "Come on, Meredith. You need a man who knows how to appreciate you. Let me get you a drink and maybe you can recover from this octopus of a boss." Scott steered Meredith back to the bar, where dozens of people were still lined up for drinks, but he finagled his way to the head of the line and persuaded the bartender to mix two Scotches.

"This is too strong," Meredith protested, wrinkling her nose.

"I'll get you some wine, then," Scott answered, tossing down his own drink. "Let me have yours. No sense letting it go to waste." He reached for Meredith's glass and took a sip, then turned back to the bartender and asked for a wine cooler.

"Scott, how can you drink so much so fast?"

"Practice," he answered with an easy grin.

It was true that Scott could drink a great deal before the effects ever began to show. But Meredith suspected that all that liquor affected him, even though it took a long time for his intoxication to become noticeable. "I'm tired, Scott, let's find someplace to sit down."

Meredith headed toward the far end of the ballroom, well away from the bar, and collapsed onto one of the folding chairs that lined the wall. Scott pulled a chair close beside hers and draped his arm across her shoulders.

"You sure look pretty tonight," he whispered. Meredith glanced down at her wool dress, a bright cinnamon color that she loved. She had worn the dress at least a hundred times, probably a dozen of them on dates with Scott, and every time she wore it, he said the same thing. She smiled at him and patted his cheek, but moved her chair slightly away from his. Scott was a dear, and she valued his friendship, she realized, glancing at his profile. He was nice looking in a quiet way, and always good company. She could count on him to be an undemanding escort, though sometimes there was a look in his eye that told her he wished for something more in their relationship. But spending time with him was like being with a cousin. He never caused her heart to beat any faster the way—

She must not think of Warren. Her imagination filled in any gaps in her actual knowledge, and she felt sure that he was quite involved with Bettis Langley. Besides, his rejection of her at the moment of surrender had bruised her ego. She was furious with herself for revealing her desire to him, and she was furious with him for rebuffing her. Her only consolation was that Warren would never know whom he had resisted on Halloween night.

Scott's arm moved down her back, but her chair was now far enough away to make the position uncomfortable. He gave up and took her hand. "You sure looked nice on TV," he said. "I watched you on the monitor."

"I was so embarrassed. I didn't know they were filming," Meredith protested. "Bettis asked me a question, and the next thing I knew, I was a celebrity," she said, laughing at herself. "It was fun, though."

"Rocky should have put you on his TV spots," Scott replied. "You're a lot more photogenic than that ugly mug of his. You would have doubled his vote."

Meredith's laughter pealed. "And to think I spent all that time on phone calls trying to get just a hundred more votes!"

"Do you think Rocky's going to win?" Scott queried.

Meredith's brow wrinkled. "I don't know. It's going

to be such a close race. I'll be glad when the votes are counted . . . I think." Her stomach gave a little lurch of anticipation. Tension was beginning to build in the room, and Meredith felt the same uneasiness as the rest of the campaign workers. They had worked very hard, and they all felt a few more days would have put them over the top. Tonight, though, nobody could call it. There were so many if's. . . .

A cheer across the room announced the news that the first ballot box was in and the votes counted. It had been a sure precinct, and Rocky had won easily. Meredith stood and cheered, too, although she knew that the tale would be told much further down the line, in the old-guard counties where money and power, not democracy, often controlled politics. She settled back into her chair and sipped her wine, only halfway listening to Scott talk about last night's football game between the Cowboys and the Rams.

The noise in the hotel ballroom had become deafening as the tension continued to mount and the crowd of people talked louder and louder in their excitement. The race ran neck and neck as Rocky and his opponent alternately overtook one another with votes from their respective areas of strength. At one point they were seven votes apart, and Meredith let out her breath with a sigh. This was nerve-racking. She hoped Rocky wouldn't lose by only seven votes. She would never forgive herself, thinking that if only she had called eight more people, got eight more votes, he would have won. She twisted the lapis beads around her neck. Worry beads, she thought. Or prayer beads. She raised her eyes to the ceiling. It couldn't hurt. Please, Lord, she said silently . . .

Scott excused himself to go to the bar and Meredith joined a nearby group while he was gone. There was an easy camaraderie in this crowd of people. Though most of them were strangers, they had worked together for a common goal and thus were bound together by something bigger than themselves.

A ripple of excitement spread through the crowd. Word had come that Rocky would join his supporters momentarily. The last precincts were being counted, and Rocky was behind by 93 votes. Fifteen more minutes and they would know who had won. Meredith stopped sipping her wine cooler and gulped it down.

The cheers became hoarse cries, and the brass band blared Rocky's theme song. Overhead thousands of brightly colored helium-filled balloons floated to the ceiling, and the crowd began stamping and clapping and thrusting their campaign posters upward in time to the music. In the midst of the hoopla the crowd parted to let Rocky through, exultant and proud, if not yet victorious. Surrounding him were his closest political advisers, including Warren Baxter. Rocky strode to the podium, a brilliant smile on his otherwise undistinguished face.

"Thank you, thank you," he cried, but his voice couldn't be heard over the roar of the crowd. Although he waved his arms for silence, his supporters ignored his request and continued to cheer, lost in the joy of their own screams. He tapped the podium again and again, to no avail, then gave up in total abandon, sharing their excitement. The television monitor then did what Rocky had been unable to do: the announcer's statement that the last ballot-box had been counted brought an instant hush. Rocky had carried the last precinct in Hutchinson County, way up in the Panhandle, by 2483 votes to 1914, making up the 93 votes he was behind and giving him a narrow victory. But it was a *victory* and his enthusiastic supporters went berserk at the news.

If the ballroom had been noisy before, now it was total bedlam. Meredith found herself being passed from person to person, hugging and pounding backs, and in her joy she found tears trickling down her cheeks. The band broke into "Waltz Across Texas," and Rocky capered down from the podium, leading his wife by the hand to start the dancing. They did two turns around the ballroom in a graceful, decorous waltz, and then Rocky surrendered his wife to Warren Baxter. Rocky turned to the crowd and swept a surprised silver-haired matron onto the dance floor while the crowd applauded. The governor-elect continued his way around the room, dancing a few bars and then releasing his partner to someone on the fringes, and taking another partner from the crowd. By chance he changed partners near the spot where Meredith was standing, and since she was the prettiest woman in his line of sight, Rocky flashed a happy smile and swept her into his arms.

She smiled back and matched his long, firmly guided steps. She was too excited to say anything, so surprised was she to find herself dancing with the new governor-elect of the state of Texas. She had worked in Rocky's campaign because she believed in his political platform, but she had never expected her small efforts to be rewarded in such a thrilling way.

"I saw you on television tonight," Rocky said.

"Oh, my." Meredith's eyes dropped. "I'm afraid I made quite a speech."

Rocky's laugh boomed. "That you did, little lady. I'll

have my work cut out for me, trying to live up to those ideas of yours." He dipped away and lightly released her arm, spinning her back into the crowd. "We'll talk about it later," he called over his shoulder, smiling again and reaching for a plump little butterball of a woman who squealed with delight. They drifted away, leaving Meredith alone in the crowd. Before she could locate Scott, a strong arm swept around her slim waist and she found herself looking into Warren's laughing dark eyes.

"Oh," she exclaimed. But there was no time for her to say anything else before they too were on the dance floor, waltzing across Texas with everybody else. Warren's arms tightened around her, pulling her close against him, and she smelled tobacco and spicy shaving lotion. His tanned cheek, a little scratchy from the day's growth of beard, was warm against hers. Heat from his body flowed through her, and his breath against her ear sent little shivers of excitement down her spine. Despite the sensations that his presence triggered in her body, she struggled to appear perfectly casual. Her behavior of Halloween night must not be repeated.

"You're certainly looking beautiful tonight," he said softly.

"Why, thank you," she stammered, remembering how old her cinnamon-colored dress was.

"Fact is, I think you're the prettiest woman in the whole place," he added.

"And what about Ms. Bettis Langley?" Meredith inquired, thinking of Bettis's red suit which was both businesslike and attractive.

"She doesn't have big, brown eyes like yours. If you could only have seen yourself on TV tonight, those eyes ready to spill tears of sympathy for the misguided criminals of this state."

"Oh, for heaven's sake, Warren," she sputtered. "Please, let's don't fight about that subject any more." She pulled away from his close grip, losing her urge to melt into his body.

"Hey," he said. "Come back." He pulled her even closer than before, but her body was taut. "Relax."

"How can I relax? You're trying to pick a fight, and I can't defend myself when you hold me so close." She turned her face away from his teasing grin.

"I need to hold you close so you won't have room to maneuver. I get the feeling that you'd hit me if you could move your arm into position."

Meredith laughed. "Hit a judge? Hardly. I'm sure you'd fine me for contempt of court."

"That's better," Warren said, coaxing another smile from Meredith's lips. He twirled her body one last time as the music ended. "Let's go find a drink," he said. "It's hot in here with so many people, and I'm thirsty." His fingers gripped hers as he led her through the crowd. The bartender recognized Warren and promptly took his order, ignoring the people in line ahead of him.

"Well, rank certainly has its privileges," Meredith said, both impressed and irritated that Warren had gotten such speedy service.

Warren ignored her sarcasm. "Let's drink to big, brown eyes and honey-blonde hair," he said, toasting her glass.

"That may be all right for you, but what about me?" she retorted. There was something in his grin that could be dangerous, and Meredith was trying to keep up her guard.

"I'll get my hair bleached first thing in the morning."

Meredith laughed. "It's too dark. It would never bleach out."

"At least I have brown eyes."

"Black." Meredith looked into the dark depths of Warren's eyes and quickly glanced away. There were fires burning there, and she knew if her eyes lingered, she would be scorched. The muscles in her throat tightened and she swallowed hard. His tanned finger walked up her sleeve, brushed her cheek, toyed with a wisp of hair near her ear. She swallowed again. Her throat was dry.

He lifted her glass to her lips. "Drink something. It's easier that way."

She sipped the champagne he had brought her. He was right. It was easier to swallow now. She took another sip of the champagne, and another. Anything to keep from looking into those dark eyes. She drained the glass.

"Want some more?" His gaze dared her. He knew why she drank the champagne so fast. The teasing was gone now.

"Why, yes. It's delicious." She was trying to act normally, but her fingers shook on the stem of the glass and a trembling sensation spread through her body. She would get hold of herself while he went to get her another drink. Her head would clear if she could just get her breath, but she couldn't do that while he stood so close to her, caressing her with his eyes.

"Here, take mine. I haven't touched it." He exchanged glasses with her.

"Don't you want some?" she asked, her voice breathless.

"I don't need any. You've already gone to my head." His voice shook slightly on the last syllable. Meredith felt her knees collapsing and reached behind her to support herself with the wall. Warren lifted the glass to her lips and she drank eagerly. Somewhere in her head Roman candles exploded, and her breath became fast and shallow. His finger touched her lips to remove a drop of champagne, then touched it to his own mouth. "Meredith," he whispered.

She set the glass down on a small table. She was too weak to hold it any longer. Their eyes held, locked, devoured. Desire surged through her, responding to the passion she saw in Warren's eyes. Her body swayed toward his, incomplete and longing.

"I want you," he said simply.

"Oh, Warren," she answered, her breath quickening. Their bodies did not touch, yet in the joining of their eyes there was a union of souls. There was no asking for a surrender, yet a surrender was made, each to the other, each aching with longing, eager to give and to receive.

"Let's get out of here," he said, his voice husky with emotion. "I want to kiss you." He led her downstairs away from the crowd and started across the red flowered carpet in the lobby, weaving around the knee-high brass planters. At the eastern end of the lobby he led her behind one of the huge pillars into the shadows which offered a reasonable degree of privacy.

"Come here," he murmured, pulling her into his arms. His head moved downward, his lips ready to claim hers. Her heart pounded against his chest, and she tilted her head for his kiss, opening her lips to his exquisite probing. The heat of his tongue brought hers to life, stroking and caressing with gentle thrusts. Light-headed, she clung dizzily to him for support, held upright only by his firm male strength against her body. It did not seem necessary to breathe. She wanted no breath that did not come from him, and her mouth demanded life from his, quivering in electric response to his wayward tongue.

"Meredith, Meredith," he whispered, "my beautiful little slave girl."

His mouth was so intoxicating that it was several seconds before Meredith realized what Warren had said. Even when the words began to register in her mind, her body tried to shut them out, melting into his with a will of its own, almost past the point of reason—*almost* past reason, but not quite.

". . . slave girl?" she murmured, still not aware of the significance of the words. His words seemed to echo from a bottomless pit until finally they penetrated her consciousness. He knew. He had known all along. She separated her mouth from his.

"How did you know?" she asked.

Warren's hands reached to pull her back into his arms. In the shadows she could see that the passion still blazed in his dark eyes. "Doesn't matter," he murmured. "Come back."

She leaned against him, but for a different kind of support this time. "How did you know?" she whispered against his ear.

Neither of them saw Scott Palmer walk up beside the post.

"I'd know that body anywhere," Warren said, responding to Meredith's question. "Your wig didn't fool me."

Scott suddenly noticed Warren in the dim shadows

and gasped in outraged jealousy. Meredith and Warren whirled, still too caught up in their own emotions to deal with Scott's. Scott grabbed Meredith's arm. "Come on, Meredith. You're going with me," he shouted, dragging her across the floor and out the heavy wooden doors.

Chapter Five

Shocked at the sudden turn of events, Warren leaned against the post and lit a cigarette, trying to clear his head. There was no denying the powerful attraction he felt toward Meredith. Physical desire had roused him to an urgency that demanded satisfaction. And she wanted him just as much as he wanted her, that was evident from the warmth of her response. But Scott Palmer presented a complicating factor. Though Warren had heard occasional rumors linking Scott and Meredith, he had given them little credence in light of the way Meredith yielded herself to his embraces.

Her kisses were not those of a woman in love with another man.

Nonetheless, the situation was getting out of bounds, and if there was anything Warren could not tolerate, it was messy circumstances. Life should be tidy and neat, with everything in its appointed place. Scott Palmer just didn't fit into the equation. Warren breathed a disgusted oath at the memory of the angry, somewhat inebriated Scott dragging Meredith through the hotel doors. It presented one hell of a predicament. All he needed was for Scott to repeat the story to a few of his lawyer colleagues, and the juicy tidbit would make the rounds in the legal community in no time. What if the lawyers ridiculed him behind his back? It would undermine his dignity so that he could no longer preside effectively over his court. The very notion revolted him. It was too high a price, no matter how much pleasure he might otherwise take in Meredith's company. He must disentangle himself from the situation at once before it got any worse and hope that when Scott sobered up, he would have sense enough not to spread the tale.

Warren crushed his cigarette and tossed it into a smoking stand, then stepped out of the shadows behind the pillar. He had lost all enthusiasm for election night, and he wasn't up to mingling with the excited campaign workers. If he went home, Meredith might call to explain or apologize and he wasn't up to that, either. Even though his mind was resolute, she was too much of a temptation to him. He needed some more time to get his desire under control. He left the Driskill, but instead of going back to his condominium, he drove east for an hour toward Bastrop and his family homeplace, now his inheritance, to spend the night.

* * *

Scott did not get many steps down the sidewalk in front of the hotel before Meredith managed to break his grip on her arm.

"Scott Palmer," she cried angrily, "just who do you think you are to pull a stunt like that? I've never been so embarrassed in my life!"

Her fiery words fell on stubborn ears. "You should be," he retorted. "It was a pretty disgusting scene."

"Disgusting! How dare you! What I do is none of your business. You don't own me!"

"Oh, ho," he said, his words slurred. "Little Meredith is ambitious for advancement, is that it? Thinks a judge can do her more good than an ordinary lawyer?"

Meredith, her face incredulous, stopped in the middle of the sidewalk. "You'd better be kidding to make a remark like that."

"Why? Looks pretty obvious to me. You gave your little speech on TV tonight, and danced with the new governor, so why not carry on a little flirtation with a judge? Can't do any harm, can it?"

"What put that crazy idea into your head?" she protested, outraged. Behind them they heard a boisterous group of campaign workers leave the hotel and start toward them. "I'm getting out of here," she said, moving down the street toward her car.

"Sure, run away," Scott cried to her retreating back. "The truth hurts, doesn't it?"

"Scott Palmer, that's despicable," she said, turning to glare at him. "I don't know what's come over you tonight, but I suggest you go home and make yourself a large pot of coffee. I only hope it's the alcohol that's making you say these insulting things." She climbed into her car, only to notice that Scott was indeed wobbly on his feet and his face was chalk-white in the light cast by the streetlight.

"Meredith, I think I'm going to be sick," he said, grabbing hold of the light pole.

"No, Scott, don't—not here," she cried, running back toward him and glancing uneasily at a group of people passing near them on the sidewalk. "You don't want it all over town that you threw up in the middle of Brazos Street." She peered into his watery eyes. "Can you hold it until I get you to my house? It won't take long."

"I don't know."

"You've *got* to . . . take deep breaths. Come on," she ordered, putting her arm around his waist and easing him into the passenger side of her car.

There was little traffic at this hour of the night, and Meredith made record time to her house. Scott's physical condition momentarily erased Meredith's anger because it was impossible for her to hate him when he was so wretched. He stretched out on her couch with a cold, wet towel over his face while she made some very strong coffee, and within a couple of hours he had sobered up.

"Meredith, I'm really sorry about the things I said earlier," he said with an expression of genuine remorse.

Meredith frowned. "They really hurt me," she answered. "You should know better than to have such ugly thoughts about me."

"I don't know what came over me," he said woefully. "Can you forgive me?"

Meredith shrugged. "Oh, sure, I can *forgive* you. The problem is going to be *forgetting* what you said."

"Look, I know it was awful for me to say it, and I

know in your case it isn't true. But it just popped into my head because stuff like that goes on all the time."

"I don't believe it," Meredith said, her voice flat.

"Don't be so naive," Scott replied. "You work in an agency with a good boss who recognizes merit and promotes people accordingly. You don't have to depend on—oh, batting your eyes and . . . being *friendly* to the right people. But out in the cold, cruel world it's different. You can thank your lucky stars you have someone like Harvey to protect you."

"Scott, do you mean that if people see me with someone prominent—like Warren Baxter, maybe—they would think I was doing it because he could be *useful* to me?"

"That's right."

Meredith felt a tide of dismay engulf her. "But, Scott, it's just not fair. I mean, nobody thinks *you're* trying to take advantage when you go out with somebody."

"Sorry you didn't know there's still a double standard in the business world. Like tonight, for instance. So what if those people saw me staggering around on the sidewalk? They'll just charge it up to high spirits on election night. But if it had been *you* staggering around like that, better believe it, your reputation would be mud."

Meredith slumped her head into her hands and glowered. No wonder Warren had misinterpreted her actions. What must he think of her after tonight? He would analyze it the same way Scott did. After all, they were both lawyers and probably thought along similar lines. She would have to explain to Warren, let him know that it wasn't like that, that her feelings were real.

She jumped up from the floor where she had been

sitting. "Come on, Scott, you've got to go home. It's late and I've got to work tomorrow." She steered Scott out the door, assuring him that of course he was forgiven but that he would be persona non grata if he overindulged in alcohol again.

As soon as Scott was safely out the door, Meredith dialed Warren's number. The telephone rang endlessly, and toward dawn she finally gave up, wondering if he had spent the night with Bettis Langley.

Meredith eventually fell asleep with a few tearstains on her pillow, and it seemed that she had scarcely dozed off when a telephone call from Harvey Gilstrap woke her with the jolting news that Diego Gutierrez had broken probation. It was always the worst part of a probation officer's job when a defendant did not live up to the terms of his probation and had to be incarcerated. It made her job seem futile when that happened, and Meredith thought life was bleak enough already. She would have to call the jail to see what Diego had done and then contact the judge who sentenced him to . . . oh, no! It was *Warren* who had sentenced Diego. Warren. She would have to go to him and concede that Diego's probation should be revoked. No. She couldn't do it. A spasm of grief shook her body, then panic rolled her out of the bed. She flew into the shower, turning on the cold water full blast, hoping her head would clear.

Promptly at eight o'clock a stern-lipped Miss Tuttle ushered Meredith and Harvey into Warren Baxter's office. By then the adrenalin generated by fear had Meredith moving in high gear. She had already gotten the information she needed from the jail and huddled with Harvey to devise a strategy which might salvage Diego's probation. Harvey was convinced their only hope was to plead for mercy.

Warren's face was grim as they went through the polite ceremony of shaking hands. His dark eyes, last night aglow with passion, were now dead embers, and he projected an attitude of aloof arrogance that should have intimidated Meredith into silence as it did Harvey. However, Meredith realized that her career as a probation officer was jeopardized and her judgment cast into doubt because of her staunch support of a probationer who had not lived up to her expectations. This time Meredith was not only pleading for Diego, she was trying to salvage her own credibility. She had carefully rehearsed a speech that would present the best face possible, but Warren's quick offensive sent her memorized set-piece spinning.

"Well, Miss Jennings, I understand that your 'poor Diego' has been caught breaking into vending machines to steal money. What lame excuse are you going to make for him this time? Let's see, is it his broken English, or his third-grade education, or his run-down shoes that sent him out with a screwdriver and pliers at 3:00 A.M.?" Warren's voice blasted with barely controlled rage. "Do you know what I think, Miss Jennings? I think your dear Diego is too weak and too lazy to function in the real world."

Meredith shot a pleading look at Harvey, who was trying to keep his eyes on the ceiling. As a plump child, Harvey had always avoided fights because it was too hard for him to defend himself; that boy had grown up and was still trying to avoid fights, though in the adult world the bouts were usually verbal rather than physical. His fear of hostilities was the source of both his strength and his weakness: he was a wonderful supervisor and negotiator because he could conciliate and harmonize a group of people; but should they refuse to be reasonable, he wanted nothing on earth so much as to escape them. At the moment he fervently wished that he could will himself into invisibility. He had never seen Judge Baxter like this before. Harvey decided he was going to ask the county commissioners for hazardous-duty pay if he lived long enough to get out of this room.

"He made an error in judgment—" Meredith attempted to placate Warren but was rudely interrupted.

"Error in judgment?" Warren uttered a cynical laugh. "I'll tell you what's really wrong with Diego, he thinks he's no good and that society wouldn't try to help him because nobody else is any good either. He has absolutely no respect for the rights of other people. He's already proved that. I should have listened to my own instincts and realized that he didn't have character enough to take advantage of an opportunity for probation. Instead I let your sad tale of woe about his hard life influence me. Just because there was a reason for what he did doesn't mean the state should excuse him. Believe me, I'll never make that mistake again. Your soft little heart can bleed all over my office, but I have a responsibility to the citizens of this county to protect them. And so do *you,* Miss Jennings. When you make a mistake, or I do, it's a threat to the entire community."

Warren's anger had driven his words like the forceful blast of a high-pressure hose. This was not the time to argue. Meredith quietly responded, "I'm sorry, Judge Baxter. Next time I'll—"

"There isn't going to be any 'next time,' Miss Jennings. Nothing like this is ever going to happen in my court again." He turned to Harvey. "Get her out of here, will you, until she grows up enough to understand human nature."

Harvey scrambled to his feet. As Meredith's supervisor he would have to share the blame for her mistake in judgment. "Well, now, Judge, our confidence wasn't completely misplaced. At least he didn't commit a violent crime."

"Not this time. But who knows what he'll do next?" Warren stood, dismissing them. "We'll have the hearing to revoke probation as soon as his lawyer can get ready. On your way out, tell Miss Tuttle to call—who's his lawyer?"

"Scott Palmer," muttered Meredith, keeping her eyes on the floor.

"Oh, yes. I'd forgotten." Warren's words were chipped from granite. "Tell Mr. Palmer I'll see him in court."

Meredith felt her whole world crumbling around her feet. Either she had been born under an unlucky star or some sinister force was taking a perverse delight in twisting the universe so that all its misery was pouring down on her. She thought she must be losing her grip. Her life had been full of problems, but always before she had been resourceful enough to deal with them as challenges rather than as obstacles. Problems had merely tested her mettle and left her stronger and more confident. But this fiasco! Fate had conspired to knot her career and her heart to the person of Warren Baxter—*Judge* Warren Baxter—and at the moment both her personal and her professional lives were being sucked down the tubes. For several days she was like an automaton, performing her tasks mechanically. Her emotions had been on such a rollercoaster ride that now she seemed to be incapable of feeling anything. She welcomed the numbness, though she was afraid it might wear off like novocaine and leave her with a throbbing heartache. She spent her days out in the field, supervising probationers on their jobs so she could get away from prying eyes at the office. The job-site visitations helped to take away some of the sting of her failure with Diego, because she was able to see defendants hard at work, making the most of their second chance. When she mentioned this to Harvey Gilstrap, he made an observation that helped her to reassess everything that had happened.

"Meredith, you've got to quit thinking it was *your* failure that caused Diego to get in trouble again. Hey, gal, can't you see it was *his* failure? *He's* the one who broke into the vending machines."

"Yes, but it might not have happened if I had known how to help him. I should have anticipated his problems."

"You can't take responsibility for the whole criminal justice system on your own shoulders. All we can do as probation officers is provide counseling and support. The probationers are the ones who have to make it work. After all, hon, it's their lives . . . and their freedom."

Harvey's words helped her set aside her guilt, and with it her depression. She could think of her job as a challenge again, rather than a hopeless task, and her desire to succeed unleashed a flood of creative energy. She found herself lying awake that night, thinking not of Warren but of ways to improve the penal system. There just *had* to be a way.

Meredith was so elated over her new plan that even the stiff-backed secretary couldn't dampen her spirits when she was ushered into the judge's office the next morning. Warren rose when Meredith walked through the door, but he did not extend his hand. And he did not smile at her. His expression was calculating, as though he expected her to try to influence him in regard to Diego Gutierrez, whose probation revocation hearing was set for the following morning.

Meredith had been about to divulge her novel idea, but a glance at his stern face caused her to reevaluate her position. She had meant to approach him as probation officer to judge, but she quickly sensed that if she were going to win his support, she would have to use strategy. She must start slowly and warm him to the idea. She would have to be absolutely professional. She cleared her throat.

"Judge Baxter, I have shared your concern about Diego Gutierrez and his failure to live up to the conditions of his probation." There, that was a safe start. Warren, however, kept his head tilted back and watched her through narrowed eyes. He nodded for her to continue. "I've checked the statistical records and found that this kind of failure occurs frequently enough that it demoralizes the probation officers and undermines the effectiveness of the probation program." There, she had managed that. It sounded so objective when it was phrased that way . . . "demoralizes the probation officers." She kept her gaze clear and direct. *Demoralizes* was such a nice, clean, *neutral* word.

"I've been wondering if we couldn't somehow get the probationers involved with the community," she continued. "Since some probationers tend to view society as an enemy force with themselves as its victims, they become hostile."

"Sociopaths would be a better term," Warren said. "Those are the people who fail. But if they could feel that they are part of the community and benefit from it, maybe they would put their efforts into striving for success rather than for revenge."

"Is revenge what Diego Gutierrez was after? Revenge because his probation officer wanted so badly for him to get a second chance that she compromised herself with the presiding judge?"

"Warren, please . . ." Because they both knew it was unfair for him to make such an inappropriate remark, Meredith refused to let it rankle her. She was committed to presenting her new plan, and she could not do that if she took exception to his words. Since he blamed her for Diego's failure, she needed very much to prove her competence to him.

She *must* control herself. She mustn't react to his harsh words. "I believe we could find jobs for these people with community agencies," she continued. "Instead of going to prison, they could 'serve time' working with the blind, or the mentally retarded, or battered women, or . . . or they could work in the parks and on road crews . . . learn new skills—"

"You make it sound like the army," he said dryly.

Nervousness made Meredith utter a thin little chuckle. But at least he was beginning to thaw.

"Well, I think you can get the picture," she said, deciding she had said enough until she had some kind of reaction from Warren.

He rubbed his eyes with his fingers, then propped his head on his hands and stared down at the desk for a long time. In the uneasy silence Meredith could hear the mechanical *rat-a-tat-tat* of the typewriter in the next room. She leaned back, crossed her slim legs, and waited.

His voice when he finally spoke was very soft, and she had to strain to listen. "Meredith, not so very long ago, when I was about your age, I was the district attorney over in Bastrop County where I grew up. It was my job to prosecute defendants who had been arrested by the sheriff and indicted by the grand jury. One of those defendants was a fellow who worked on the oil rigs. He'd gotten drunk and gotten in a fight with somebody. Raised a big ruckus. Threatened to kill the foreman for breaking up the fight. They had to get the sheriff out there because he had a knife and had taken a slice out of his opponent. Well, the other fellow pressed charges, and it was up to me to prosecute him."

Meredith found herself sitting on the edge of her chair. What had come over Warren? What did this story from his past have to do with her visit to his office this morning? She felt confused and . . . anxious. Anxious, because there was a terrible emptiness in Warren's voice. The words hovered in the air, cold and dead.

"The jury convicted him, of course. There were so many witnesses they had no other choice." Warren was lost in thought. "But he had begged me to go easy on him. Said he had a wife and kids in Arkansas who needed him, and if I'd get him probation, he'd go back and take care of them." Warren's fingers fiddled aimlessly with papers on his desk. "I knew he had a record, a long series of drunken fights, barroom brawls, threats and assaults. Nothing major. Nothing to make you expect—" He dropped the papers and leaned back in his chair. There was a faraway look in his eyes, and pain, a lot of pain. He took a deep breath and spoke very quickly. "So I recommended to the jury that they give him probation. No need to lock up a man with a wife and kids to support, I said. And the jury agreed with me. So he got a suspended sentence, and he went home to Arkansas. And before the month was out, he beat his wife to death. She was twenty-five. The kids were three and six, and they're in foster homes now. He's in prison where he ought to be. But *I* should have been the one who sent him there. His wife's blood is on my hands just the same as if I'd killed her myself."

Meredith felt a rush of sympathy that she did not know how to express. She wanted to go to him and put her arms around him, stroke his head and whisper to him that everything would be all right, but she did not dare. In this moment of revealed suffering, Warren was too fragile to touch. Raw pain etched deep lines beside his mouth, and his eyes were opaque.

"Warren, I'm so sorry," she whispered. "But you mustn't blame yourself . . ."

He struggled for self-control and won. He gave himself a mental shake. "I don't know why I bored you with that old story," he said, rising. "I'm sure you have other things to do."

"Warren," she said, wondering what had changed him. Why was he being so abrupt?

"Thank you for coming by to share your idea. It will depend on the other judges whether we would ever be able to do anything with it or not. Please don't get your hopes up, however." He spoke into the intercom. "Is my next appointment here, Miss Tuttle?"

Meredith picked up her purse and walked to the door. For a moment Warren had opened up, overcome his rigid self-control, and there was an intimacy between them. Then just as quickly it was over and he had tuned her out. Sorrow welled up in her because Warren was so afraid of being wrong or being vulnerable that he kept his emotions locked deep within. He didn't trust his own feelings, so how could he trust the feelings of anyone else? He would never again risk failure. Oh, Warren, her heart silently pleaded, life isn't worth living if you're afraid to take a chance. But she couldn't say the words aloud. He had put on his emotional armor and would not hear her.

Warren extended his hand for a hearty handshake and gave her the cordial smile of a political candidate.

Meredith sat at the oak bench in the third-floor courtroom. The procedure took very little time. Scott Palmer made a brief opening argument requesting that Diego's probation be continued and that the court overlook the burglary due to "extenuating circumstances." The prosecutor responded that the defendant had already received adequate opportunities and had failed to make any effort to rehabilitate himself. The state then introduced testimony from several witnesses to prove Diego's latest offense. The prosecutor explained that the state would not proceed to press charges on the new offense if the court would revoke probation and send the defendant to the state penitentiary to serve his one-year term for his prior offense. When Judge Baxter asked the defendant if he wished to present any testimony in his own behalf, Diego sat in sullen silence. Scott leaned forward and whispered in Diego's ear, but Diego shook his head vigorously. Then Scott stood and told the judge that the defendant had no evidence to present.

"Very well. The court revokes the probation previously granted this defendant on the charge of auto theft and sentences him to a one-year term in the state penitentiary, to begin immediately. So ordered." Warren rose, robe swirling, and left the bench. No one was close enough to him to see that his face was ashen.

A deputy sheriff walked to the counsel table with a pair of handcuffs and placed them on Diego's hands. Meredith hurried to the rail to speak to Diego, but he averted his head and followed the deputy out of the courtroom.

Before Meredith could leave the courtroom, the bailiff entered the side door and came over to her.

"Miss Jennings?" he asked. "Judge Baxter said he'd like to see you in his chambers before you leave."

Meredith's heels clicked on the marble floor as she hurried around to Warren's office. Her thoughts were in a state of utter confusion. She swept past Miss Tuttle as though she did not even exist and entered Warren's private office.

"You wanted to see me?" she asked. She noticed that he had already removed his robe and stood in his gray worsted business suit. It was an excellent fit, she thought idly, draping perfectly across his broad shoulders.

His face was a study in conflict. "Won't you sit down?" he inquired politely. "Let me get you a cup of coffee."

"Thank you, no." Surely this wasn't a social visit.

"Please have a seat," he repeated, waving toward the red leather sofa at the opposite end of the office. She sat down and he joined her, sitting in the wing chair at right angles to the sofa. His worried eyes studied her face. She was too weary to try to hide anything. She didn't know what he could read in her expression and she no longer cared. She was incapable of playing the role of poised professional in the face of all this pain—Diego's, Warren's, her own, it almost seemed the whole world's.

Don't you think you're being overdramatic? an inner

voice mocked. Really, now, a peon like you isn't capable of carrying the pain of the whole world. She felt better mulling that thought. There was nothing quite so bracing as a sense of one's own unimportance. The pain was still there, but in perspective.

Somebody had to say something. "Well, here we are again," Meredith said finally, when Warren seemed disinclined to speak.

He seemed jittery. "Now that you're here, it's a little hard to know where to start."

"I know the feeling," she murmured, remembering the night in his apartment.

"I expected you to be angry," he said.

"Angry? I'm not angry. Why should I be?"

Warren ran his fingers through his dark hair and didn't even care that he left it rumpled. "I know you wanted very badly to help Diego. I'm sorry it didn't work out."

"We tried. That's all any of us can do. He didn't do his part, that's all."

"You don't feel . . . responsible for it?" He seemed surprised.

"Not any more. I did at first." Until now they had avoided meeting each other's eyes, but their glances now met and held, searching for understanding. Meredith wondered if she dared to be honest with Warren, whether he could deal with a truthful statement of her feelings. "I felt responsible because *you* made me feel responsible. You blamed me, so I blamed myself. But Harvey helped me to see that it wasn't *my* failure, it was Diego's."

"But you were the one who recommended probation for him. Wasn't that *your* mistake?" He wasn't argumentative; he simply wanted to know.

"In a way, I suppose it was. But, Warren, I'm not perfect. If nobody can be a probation officer except someone who never makes a mistake, there aren't going to be many people left on the payroll."

"But you have a responsibility to the community."

"So I do. And I take it very seriously. I do the best I can to check the backgrounds of defendants very carefully and recommend only the ones who I feel can make it for probation. But, Warren, when you're working with people, some of them are going to let you down sometimes. *Nobody* can predict behavior with absolute certainty, not even psychiatrists. My job is to know when the risk is worth taking. I think it's important to trust people as long as it's reasonable to do so. And not very many have let me down." She tried to smile.

Warren leaned his head against the high-backed chair and pressed his fingertips against his chin. Meredith's candor was disconcerting. He did not know how to react to an open expression of emotions. It made him feel anxious, as if he should back away. He had already let down his guard with her once.

Meredith was beginning to understand this side of his nature and could sense his withdrawal. "What's the matter, Warren? Does it bother you that I said it was *you* who made me feel bad over Diego, and unnecessarily so?"

He nodded almost imperceptibly. He was ready to take control of this conversation and steer it back to safe territory.

"I know you're going to pull away just as you did yesterday," she said. "Before you get your mask back on, let me just say that I took a risk when I told you what I honestly felt. I decided to give you the same trust I would give to one of my probationers, and if you couldn't handle it, then it was your failure, not mine."

A light flashed in his eyes and he stood up and paced the room. The conversation was absurd. It was ridiculous for people to muck about with their feelings. Feelings were for—for *children,* for God's sake. Why couldn't Meredith hold back some of her irrepressible emotions? She asked for more than he could give. Wasn't their physical passion enough? He stopped pacing and lit a cigarette. It was time to end the conversation.

"I want to apologize for being too harsh on you about Diego," he said. "I disagree with your probation philosophy, but it would be unfair to hold one mistake against you. Your record is very commendable otherwise." He turned to her with a cordial smile.

"Warren, you're playing a role again. And I don't call that much of an apology."

"Sorry, but it's the best I can do at the moment."

Meredith could not repress a chuckle.

"What brought that on?" he queried.

"That's the first honest thing you've said to me since I came in this office."

He gave an abashed smile. But the tension of dealing with an emotional situation made him seek refuge in physical sensation, the only kind of feeling that did not pose a threat to him. Suddenly he wanted to pull her into his arms and hold her close. He took a step toward her. She rose from the sofa, a determined tilt to her chin.

"I know what you're thinking, Warren," she said, backing away. "But it's just too soon. We both need time to think."

"What's there to think about?" he murmured, catching her arm and pulling her against him.

"Plenty, for both of us. I'm pretty confused, and so are you. I think it would be better for us to put our personal relationship on hold for the time being while we sort things out. Okay?"

She was resolute. She went out the door without waiting for his answer.

Chapter Six

Meredith glanced for the thousandth time at the invitation to the noon inauguration propped up on her desk. For the thousandth time she changed her mind about whether or not to attend the ceremonies. She wanted to go, and she had been terribly excited when the invitation came. But Warren Baxter was sure to be prominent at the ceremonies, and Meredith had spent recent weeks carefully avoiding any contact with him. If she went, she was sure to run into him. She wasn't ready for that. Her heart wasn't ready.

After Diego's hearing, Warren had telephoned her several times, but she always made an excuse not to see him and soon he stopped calling. There had followed a long silence, until last week on New Year's Eve. She had declined several party invitations because she was not in a party mood. At midnight the telephone had rung, and Meredith had answered with a muffled "Hello." At the other end of the line Meredith heard Warren's low voice saying, "I just wanted to wish you Happy New Year, Meredith." In the noisy background Meredith heard a female voice cry, "Where are you, Warren? I want my New Year's kiss." Then the telephone had gone dead, and Meredith had felt a devastating loneliness.

Though she understood Warren better than she had previously, she knew she could not change him. He wanted a relationship that was limited to the physical, without any emotional ties. Emotions posed a threat to his self-control. And Meredith knew herself only too well. She knew that she could not have a relationship with him without becoming emotionally involved. Her nature was too passionate. Thus Warren was a dilemma to her: she felt an overpowering desire for him when she was with him, yet she feared the heartbreak that was inevitable if she let herself become involved with someone who seemed emotionally paralyzed.

Over the weeks she had attempted to subdue any thought of Warren. She knew she could pull her life back together, given enough time . . . but was she ready to test herself this soon? On the other hand, she had worked hard in Rocky Rockwell's campaign, and she wanted to watch him take the oath of office as governor of Texas. . . . She made up her mind to go to the inauguration.

Fortunately, today she had worn a kelly green wool suit she had bought as a Christmas present to herself, adding a white blouse trimmed with lace which her mother had sent her from Houston, and felt very dressed up. Meredith walked briskly to Harvey Gilstrap's office and told him she wanted to take leave time for the rest of the morning so she could go over to the capitol to watch the inauguration. She was glad she hadn't scheduled any probation visits and could leave with a clear conscience.

"Would you like to go, too?" she asked Harvey. "I'm going to call Scott and see if he'll come by for me." Still uneasy at the prospect of seeing Warren, Meredith thought that she'd feel more secure if she had plenty of company.

"Might as well," Harvey answered, pleased to be invited.

Scott met them in front of the building, and they walked quickly down Eleventh Street in the gray January mist. The cold air brought color to Meredith's cheeks, and the men offered sincere compliments on how attractive she looked in her suit. Lighthearted, they walked three abreast down the street past the Governor's Mansion and crossed over to the pink granite capitol building. They looked up at the capitol dome, patterned after the classic style of the nation's capitol in Washington, D.C., and Meredith felt a rush of happiness that she had a good job in an exciting city where she could be part of government and help to make the state a better place in which to live.

They were carried along in the flow of the crowd and found a place where they could see some of the ceremony by standing on tiptoe and peering over the heads in front of them. The Chief Justice of the Texas Supreme Court delivered the oath in a deep voice that was properly solemn for the occasion, then gave Rocky a hearty handshake. There were various speeches, including one by the new governor himself, and when it was finished the news media swarmed around the important officials, hoping to capture an inside story or a choice anecdote. Meredith noticed that Bettis Langley had cornered the governor and his wife. Leave it to her, Meredith thought, to get an interview with the most important person of all. And, of course, Warren was standing right beside her.

Meredith's bright green suit stood out in the crowd, and Warren recognized her even at a distance. He had thought he might see her here today, since he knew that all the campaign volunteers had been invited to the inauguration. Her excuses on the telephone had been irritating to him, and at the same time intriguing. No woman had ever turned him down before. In his more cynical moments he wondered if she were playing "hard to get," but then quickly realized that she was one of the most sincere people he had ever met.

She had said they needed time to think, that they were confused. He really couldn't understand her attitude. He felt no confusion at all. He wanted to make love to her and she wanted to make love to him—so why fight it? What was there to think about?

The light shimmered on Meredith's hair as she turned to speak to someone in the crowd. He smiled. Just wait, Meredith Jennings, he thought. Before this day is over, I'm going to back you into a corner so you can't escape, and we'll just see how long you'll resist. With a jaunty spring in his step he started through the crowd in pursuit.

Meredith and her two escorts fought their way through the crowds back out onto the capitol steps and stood, chatting idly, in the damp breeze. Meredith reached up and gingerly stroked her blonde hair, checking to see if it had begun to frizz the way it usually did in the Austin humidity. Meredith had never been vain about her looks, and was so totally unself-conscious that she was often surprised when she received a compliment. But frizzy hair drove her crazy, even though there was nothing she could do about it. It went with the damp weather. Still, in the unlikely event she should bump into Warren, she did not want him to see her at a disadvantage. After all, he had seen Bettis Langley looking TV-glamorous in a dress the color of winter violets that set off her ivory skin and dark hair.

"What time do you have to go back to work?" Scott asked. "Do we have time to go over to the governor's mansion for the reception?"

"I'm going back to work," Harvey muttered. "I can't push through another crowd. You two run along. You may be lucky enough to get a glass of champagne."

There were literally fountains of champagne flowing freely from abundant sources. The governor's supporters had seen to it that there was money enough to do him proud at his reception. Neiman-Marcus had been commissioned to do the hors d'oeuvres, and beautifully sculpted tidbits had been flown in early that morning from Dallas. Meredith tasted her first Russian caviar—which she could easily live without—and her first pâté de foie gras—which she adored. Scott was quite taken with the *mousse de Canard* and the escargots, but Meredith decided to pass. The steak tartare, however, was another matter. So highly seasoned it burned her mouth, it nonetheless kept beckoning her back for more.

"What's in this?" she asked.

"The hottest peppers in Texas," Scott answered, declining the choice bite she offered him. "They're so hot they cook the meat."

"You mean it isn't cooked?"

"Nope." He chuckled at Meredith's look of dismay. "But it's very choice sirloin. Have some more, why don't you?"

Meredith popped another bite into her mouth, but this time it didn't taste so good. "Try some of the lobster soufflé," he suggested. "It's perfect."

Bettis Langley appeared with a camera crew to photograph the tables laden with delicacies. The governor's wife explained to the television audience that they had decided to have a gourmet reception to let the world know that Texas didn't consist exclusively of barbecued beef and Lone Star beer. She was quick to add, however, that they expected to have many barbecues at the mansion since Rocky was a world-class cook when it came to barbecued spareribs. Bettis probably added ten points to the Channel 36 ratings when she got Mrs. Rockwell's promise to make available Rocky's barbecue-sauce recipe to anyone who wrote the station asking for it. Meredith had to admire Bettis's finesse. She could find an unusual angle on the most ordinary-seeming interview. Bettis's savvy made Meredith feel gauche in contrast. She turned to Scott and suggested they get in line to shake hands with the governor, who was due to start receiving guests at any moment. She wanted to get away from Bettis and her fluid ease in handling people and situations.

They passed the time chatting with friends and acquaintances nearby in the receiving line. There was an atmosphere of excitement, increased by the presence of television crews and the superb food and drink. Meredith considered herself well-paid for the hundreds of telephone calls she had made in Rocky's behalf. Some of these people had contributed only money; she had contributed part of herself, through her efforts, and she basked in the glow of the reward for a job well done.

Eventually they worked their way to the front of the line, and Meredith introduced herself to Rocky and his wife. Rocky, who could recall faces even though names sometimes escaped him, recognized Meredith from her television interview on election night. He turned to his wife with some complimentary remarks that warmed Meredith's heart. The man really had a gift for making people feel special, she thought. She smiled in appreciation, and before she could move on, Warren stepped from his position farther down the receiving line and clapped the governor on the back.

"You remember Miss Jennings, don't you?" he interrupted. "She's one of our probation officers in Travis County. She has an idea for a new approach to probation that you really ought to let her explain to you sometime soon."

Rocky had turned in surprise at the sound of Warren's voice in his ear, but when he looked back at Meredith and her fresh good looks, he thought he understood. There was an interesting gleam in Warren's eye that might explain his interest in Meredith's career. . . . Still, Warren never promoted the work of anyone who wasn't top-flight. "Very fine," Rocky answered, as Meredith and Scott were swept on down the line. "I'll have my administrative assistant contact you very soon. Penal reform is high on my list of priorities."

Scott pinched Meredith's elbow. "Can you believe that, Meredith?" he asked, awed. "What a break for you!"

Meredith's fingers were cold as she continued to

shake hands and smile at the important personages in the receiving line. Her eyes had met Warren's for only a split second, and that had been enough to set her heart to racing. Her emotions were so stirred by his presence that she had scarcely heard a word Rocky had said. "Wha—what did you say?" she stammered to Scott.

"Your career," he answered, grinning. "This is your big chance. To get to explain a project to the governor himself! What I wouldn't give for a chance like that!"

Meredith heard the sound of Scott's voice but his words did not penetrate her consciousness. She glanced back over her shoulder to find Warren watching her, a devilish grin on his face. Why did he make a pitch for her with the governor? And why did he look so pleased with himself?

Meredith's mind was whirling. All the feelings she had submerged for the past few weeks were springing to the surface. She *knew* Warren would disturb her—that's why she had stayed away from him, why she had brought Scott along to protect her. She grimaced at Scott's familiar shape beside her, realizing too late that he would be no protection at all with Warren around. Warren's presence was too . . . unsettling. The currents that passed between them traveled on their own invisible network of power lines, and Scott was hopeless as either lightning rod or shock absorber. The full force of Warren's sexual energy was directed at Meredith, and her heart did crazy things when she saw him standing near.

She broke away from the line and headed for the terrace, Scott trailing her steps. She had to get outside and get some air. She was suffocating. She had been kidding herself these past weeks when she thought she had slowly stifled her feelings for Warren. All it took was one look and they sprang to life with all their original fervor. She sank onto a wrought-iron bench and fanned her face, flushed bright pink. "It's too warm in there," she murmured. Any excuse, quickly. "So many people."

Scott's eyes expressed genuine concern. "Too much excitement, you mean."

Her eyes were stricken. How had he guessed? She had told him nothing of her feelings for Warren. "Excitement?" she croaked.

"The governor. I still can't believe how lucky you are. All the things you've been wanting to do for so long, and now you'll have your chance."

Meredith slipped out of her jacket and let the cool air blow over her. She felt as if she had a low-grade fever, and she now welcomed the same damp breeze that had caused her earlier complaints because it frizzed her hair. Thank heaven Scott had not guessed the real reason for her behavior.

"You'd better put your jacket back on," he insisted. "You'll catch a cold with nothing but that wisp of a blouse."

"Give me a few more minutes. I thought I was going to faint, it got so warm inside the mansion." She would just pretend it was the crowds.

"Please, Meredith. Put your jacket back on, and I'll go get you some punch or champagne. That'll cool you off."

"Will you, Scott? That would be so nice." Wonderful, in fact, if he would just leave her alone for a few minutes and let her pull herself back together. She put her jacket back on.

"You stay right here," he admonished her. "I'll never find you in all this crowd if you move."

"I'll be right here when you get back, don't worry." Her berry-colored lips formed a smile and Scott disappeared, a gallant knight eager to rescue a damsel in distress.

Before Meredith could take even one breath, she was astonished to find herself gazing upward into Warren's rugged face, his dark eyes ablaze. Her voice sounded tinny and breathless in her own ears, but she squeaked out a word of thanks for the opportunity he had created for her with the governor.

"It's nothing," he said, idly waving his hand, dismissing her thanks. "I'm always glad to help someone with talent. Besides," he added, "it's always a pleasure to do a favor for a beautiful woman. I'm . . . at your service."

Meredith's pulse pounded in her throat. Again she felt that she might suffocate if she didn't get some air. She looked around at the terrace, crowded with dozens of people. There was no privacy at all. She needed to tell Warren that he had to stay away from her, that their passion could lead only to heartbreak—for her, at least. But there were too many people here for such a personal conversation. She would surely be overheard. And how could she even speak, with her heart all aflutter? His presence was . . . intoxicating. The stirrings of desire sent a rosy blush to her cheeks, and again she felt a warmth spread through her body. She struggled to remove her jacket again and found that she had made a terrible mistake. Warren's strong fingers closed on her shoulder.

"I'll help you with that," he said, his voice very even. He was pleased to see that her resistance was breaking down. She was afraid to meet his eyes, and he felt the sense of victory.

"That's all right. Maybe I'll keep it on." But no, she couldn't—it was too hot. She slipped it off one shoulder, fanning her face with her other hand.

Warren's hand grasped the soft flesh above her elbow, lifting her from her chair. He had enjoyed the pursuit, but his desire now hungered for more than games.

"Wha—?"

"Let's just take a little walk in the fresh air," he said, his words slow and deliberate. "You look ill."

"I can't leave," she protested hoarsely. "Scott—"

"—can go to the devil," he responded firmly. "Come on." He steered her through the clusters of animated guests.

"No," she repeated. "He won't be able—"

"Of course not. That's the whole idea."

She whirled and looked into his face, then quickly looked away. His eyes were molten lava, devouring her. She would be mummified like the people at Pompeii when the volcano erupted, and nobody would ever know what happened to her. Her lungs gasped for air.

"What's wrong, Meredith?" he whispered, raising his hand to touch her forehead. Again the slow smile. "You seem to have a fever."

"I'm fine, really." Really. Fine. Or she would be, if only the terrace would quit spinning. Panic surged through her and she turned to run.

She reckoned without the iron clasp of his hand on her wrist. She plunged down the steps off the terrace and onto the north lawn, Warren beside her.

"Stay away from me," she whispered, her voice desperate.

He tossed back his head and laughed. He was thoroughly enjoying her discomfort. She was so weak that her knees were buckling. "You've run as far as you're going to run, Meredith. This time I've got you."

"Scott . . ." she cried weakly.

"Forget that Boy Scout," Warren said. "You need a man, Meredith."

"No, you're wrong," she insisted in a shaky voice. "I need someone who can show his feelings and be as open with me as I am with him."

Warren gave her a knowing look. "I think my feelings are quite obvious. There's no question in your mind what I'm thinking."

She blushed. "There's more to it than just . . . sexual attraction."

"Not when the attraction is this strong," he objected. "We're adults. We know what we're doing. Nobody is going to get hurt."

"*I* might."

"I'm not going to hurt you, Meredith."

"You wouldn't do it intentionally. It's just the way I am. We're different."

He laughed. *"Vive la différence."*

They had conversed oblivious to cars passing by on Colorado Street, unmindful of the crowds of people swarming the Governor's Mansion behind them. But when a loud clap of thunder reverberated across the sky, followed by a sudden burst of raindrops, their attention was deflected to the sky.

"Damn!" Warren's irritation was severe. He bent his head against the rain and turned up the collar to his suit. "Even the heavens are against us!"

"Don't stand there talking," Meredith said with a rueful laugh. "We'll get soaked." She turned and ran lightly down the street, Warren close behind her. Over her shoulder she cried, "I hope my new suit doesn't get ruined. It's wool, and I'm afraid it might shrink."

Warren looked down dismally at his own wool business suit, new for the inauguration, now sprinkled with raindrops. He put on a burst of speed and ran past Meredith. "Come on, slowpoke, before the sky really turns loose."

They stepped over puddles, hurrying across Eleventh Street. The sky, gray and sodden, pelted them with stinging raindrops, and they heard another low rumble of thunder. Warren reached out for Meredith's hand and pulled her into the doorway of the closest shelter, a white brick office building. They stood in the niche, protected now from the rain, and Warren pulled Meredith into his arms.

"Warren, don't," she protested, pulling away from him. "People will see us." She gestured to the traffic in the street. "We should be more careful." Meredith looked away from the invitation in Warren's eyes. "It wouldn't be any good for either one of us. You know how everybody at the courthouse loves to gossip." The prospect of becoming the subject of whispered innuendos had a dampening effect on Meredith's desire. She stepped away from Warren and told him to behave himself.

"I can't. You drive me mad with passion." He took her hand in his and held it to his heart. "Feel that," he said, pantomiming a heart pounding so wildly it shook her hand with the force of its vibrations. Meredith giggled.

"You sound like a little girl when you giggle like that," he teased.

Something prodded Meredith's back and she jumped out of the way of the door opening behind her. A stunning redhead in a khaki-colored raincoat stepped onto the stoop with them. "Excuse me," the redhead said, glancing with interest at the male half of the couple. "Why, hello there, Judge Baxter," she added in surprise.

"Hello, Sondra," he replied. "How are things around your office today?"

"In total chaos, as usual. And you might know that as soon as it started raining, Bernie just had to have his motion filed. Well, here goes. . . ." She stepped off the stoop and hurried down the street with a long-legged stride, making a mental note to find out who the cute blonde was. At coffee break Sondra could report another Baxter conquest.

"Meredith," Warren whispered when they were alone again, pulling her against his body and pressing her head to his chest. For a long time he simply held her, saying nothing, while they waited for the rain to stop. Meredith was afraid to look up at him. She could feel that funny, suffocating feeling starting in her throat again. Her heart pounded from pumping blood so furiously, and there was a deafening roar in her ears.

The rain slowed and became gentle, scattered drops again.

"Hey," Warren cried, "let's get out of here while the rain has stopped." He seized Meredith's wrist and together they ran down the street toward the Stokes Building. The clouds opened for another brief burst of moisture, and Warren pulled Meredith into the shelter of the nearby AFL-CIO Building until the rain stopped again. What was normally a five-minute walk to the capitol building took nearly forty-five minutes for the return trip. When they reached the parking garage next to the Stokes Building, Meredith disengaged herself to get her Volkswagen.

"I'm going to have to go home and change clothes before I can go back to work," she said. "I can't go in the office looking like a wreck." She vainly attempted to fluff her blonde hair, damp now and plastered to her head.

"Want me to take you?" Warren asked. "I'll go get my car over at the courthouse parking garage."

"No." Meredith's fingers were trembling as she unlocked the door to the driver's side.

"Why not?"

Meredith averted her head. "I don't need you around while I dry my hair and change clothes."

"I'll buy your lunch."

"I had plenty to eat at the inauguration."

"I'll hold the blow-dryer for you."

"No."

"I think you're trying to avoid me, Meredith."

"Oh, I am. I certainly am." She opened the car door.

His hand on her shoulder stopped her before she could climb in. "Why?"

She looked into his eyes and quickly looked away. "I'm scared of you."

"Of *me?*" He caught her chin and held her head still so she couldn't look away. "Be honest."

There was a long silence. Meredith could feel Warren's breath against her cheek. Her lips twisted in a doleful smile. "You're right. I'm afraid of myself." Her breath was shallow.

Warren's other hand moved up to cup her face. "Tell me why, Meredith."

"I can't." She tried to avert her head, but she was too slow. His lips came down and closed upon hers. His mouth, warm and tasting of champagne, gently explored hers, searching out its delicious hollows and recesses. His tongue flicked and darted, teasing hers to respond . . . begging hers to respond . . . daring hers to respond.

The passion which had taken weeks to beat down was

rekindled in an instant, and her tongue sparked with fire caught from his, wild and wanton as it quivered against his, then pulled back, playfully teasing his to follow. His teeth nipped at her full bottom lip but there was no pain, only pleasure of the most exquisite kind. Her teeth nibbled in return, delighting in the salty taste of his flesh. She twisted her head back and parted her lips, begging him to enter, to feast and to feed. Her body strained against his, her breasts yearning with desire. Against her ear Meredith could hear Warren's ragged breathing and a soft moan trembled in her throat.

His lips brushed against the hollow of her neck and lingered. A shudder of desire spread through her. His lips moved up, nibbled at the lobe of her ear, then gently swept across her eyelids. His hand moved down, massaged her shoulder, moved underneath her jacket to cup her breast. "So soft," he whispered, almost to himself. His mouth moved, warm and hungry, into the secret hollow of her neck. Delicious quiverings of longing coursed through her body. His lips pressed into her soft skin, eager to experience her taste, her warmth. "I want you, Meredith." His hand stroked her breast.

"Oh, Warren," she whispered. She flung her arms around his neck and drew his mouth down to hers.

His hand left her breast and moved back to brush her cheek. She turned her head and found his fingers with her warm lips.

"Warren," she whispered again, catching his hand and moving it back to her waiting breast. His finger caressed gently, but only for a moment, then moved across to stroke her other breast until it tingled with excitement.

She looked up, her pupils dilated, into the powerful

mastery of his will, and surrendered. She could not resist him any longer. Desire had overcome her better judgment. "Take me home," she said with a soft moan.

He pulled her into his arms, fierce and demanding. His mouth came down and seized possession of hers, devouring with a hunger that was beyond passion. His breath rasped against her ear, and she felt his body surge with desire. "Meredith, Meredith," he whispered, over and over, his lips assaulting hers, demanding entry, her lips responding with the same reckless urgency. His hands explored her body, eager to know its secrets. "Let's get out of here." He blindly nudged her into the car, bending over to continue kissing her.

"Hey! What's going on over there?" a strange voice cried, echoing from the other side of the building. "Miss Jennings, are you okay? Stop or I'll shoot!"

Hurried footsteps pounded on the cement. Meredith and Warren whirled, but their eyes, dilated with passion, could not focus in the semi-darkness of the parking building. "Wha—" Warren said, his hand still intimately touching Meredith's breast.

"Miss Jennings, are you okay?" shouted Rusty Weaver, the retired deputy sheriff who worked as a guard at the state offices to supplement his Social Security check. "Let go of her, you—" Rusty shone his high-beam flashlight in their faces and backed away in sudden embarrassment when he recognized Warren. "I'm sorry, Judge—excuse me . . . didn't know it was you. Sorry, Judge." Rusty turned and ran as fast as his seventy-year-old legs would carry him.

Chapter Seven

Rumors spread through the courthouse like a prairie fire. Everywhere Meredith went she was the object of curious stares and knowing smirks. Mortified to her very soul, Meredith attempted to hold her head high so that no one would guess her discomfiture. Yet every time she walked into the coffee lounge and heard all conversation stop, she knew her face flamed with an embarrassment that she could not hide. It was painfully obvious to her that for the time being she had lost all credibility as a probation officer. No one was interested in her work; they were interested only in speculating about her private life—which had become glaringly *public,* she thought despairingly.

Quite by coincidence Governor Rockwell summoned Meredith to the state capitol for the promised conference on her rehabilitation program. Impressed with her ideas, he appointed her to a state-wide committee on penal reform—a committee staffed with the most prestigious of the state's judges, attorneys, and decision-makers. What should have been the proudest moment of her career was turned into a mockery by the spiteful innuendos of jealous colleagues. Not satisfied with suggestive speculation about Meredith's personal relationship with Warren, these people now indulged in idle rationalizations about her professional status. The story spread that Warren had boosted Meredith's career as a payoff for sexual favors, and it seemed that nobody was willing to credit her advancement to professional expertise. She knew if the situation didn't change quickly and drastically, her position on the state committee would become a sham, and she would lose credibility with the other members.

Desperate to be taken seriously and to reestablish her role as a serious-minded probation officer, Meredith spent many sleepless nights trying to devise a workable strategy. She *had* to salvage her career somehow. Everything she had worked for hung tantalizingly just beyond her reach. The appointment to the state committee was her big break, her chance not only to prove herself, but also to achieve the innovations which she hoped would effect a worthwhile improvement in the state's penal system. How dare the other committee members ridicule her suggestions! And how dare her own colleagues assume the worst about her relationship with Warren! True, she and Warren hadn't behaved in the most sensible way that afternoon, but still . . .

At this point her thoughts always stopped short. The memory of Warren's demands and her passionate response was too vivid, too disturbing. She wanted Warren—oh, how she wanted him—yet he was now as far removed from her as if he had been on another planet.

Rusty's flashlight on Inauguration Day had doused Warren's passion as effectively as a cold shower. Warren had bundled Meredith into her car and sent her home to change clothes, saying that they could not take a chance on being seen leaving together. He promised to call her from his apartment as soon as he had changed—and he did call. But the intervening twenty minutes had completely changed his attitude. He was furious with himself for having put Meredith in a compromising position. He was even more upset at his lack of self-control. He had let his desires overmaster his judgment and now he and Meredith would both have to pay the consequences.

Warren knew how county government operated. It was a small world unto itself, and behavior that might pass unnoticed in a different milieu was exaggerated by courthouse gossip. Eventually the talk would die down, but for now, all eyes would be upon them. By the time Warren called Meredith, he had recovered his iron-willed control.

"I think it would be best if we didn't see each other for a while," he said, his voice distant and angry.

"Oh . . . well, perhaps that's best," she said, her heart sinking.

Warren steeled himself not to respond to the hurt in her voice. He would not let his feelings for her overpower him again. "Everyone will be watching us," he said, "so we need to avoid each other as much as possible. If we're discreet, I think the storm will die down."

"Well, then . . ." Why was his voice so icy? Was he mad at *her* for what had happened? But she dared not ask. "Will you . . . call me sometime?"

"Not for a while," he said tersely. What was the use of calling when he couldn't see her? He would just want her the more. It would have to be a clean break so they could both get on with their lives.

He wasn't going to call. It was over. He had retreated into his shell again, just as he had done before. Meredith felt numb with shock. Within a half hour they had gone from the heights of passion to this cold finality. She whispered goodbye and hung up the telephone.

Sometimes she ran into Warren—it was inevitable because of their jobs—but he always kept a safe distance. If circumstances required it, he would nod politely, but there was never a smile for her. Sometimes she thought she must have dreamed his passionate kisses. Certainly there was no hint in this aloof, arrogant judge that he had ever whispered his desire and demanded her response. His face was now as cold and hard as if it had been chiseled from ice. Apparently he felt contempt for her. She was humiliated but refused to show it. He must never know how much he had made her despise herself.

Even Scott was unable to comfort her. She never mentioned the gossip, and he was too tactful to bring it up himself. There were too many stories for him to believe nothing had happened between Meredith and Warren, but he was unsure how intimate they had been. It was a mess, any way you looked at it. Scott even found himself the butt of crude jokes, since everybody had taken it for granted that Meredith was Scott's "girlfriend" after two years of off-and-on dating. Scott thought he would punch out the next man who walked up to him, slapped him on the shoulder, and gave him a sympathetic glance. Scott sometimes felt annoyed with Meredith for making them the objects of ridicule, but poor kid, she was so miserable herself that all Scott could do was try to stand by her and weather the storm. Surely in time it would all blow over. In the meantime . . .

In the meantime Meredith thought she would die of mortification. Hardly a day went by that someone did not razz her about Rusty's tale. Her associates meant only to tease her, but her blushes gave an added incentive to keep the story alive. Harvey grumbled at people from time to time, but human nature being what it was, the more they were forbidden to talk, the more they talked—they just waited until Harvey was safely out of the office.

"Hey, Meredith, bring your coffee over here," called Oliver Leachman. "We want to hear about the inauguration. The rest of us weren't lucky enough to get an invitation."

A red color spread up Meredith's neck and cheeks. This had gone far enough. "The rest of you didn't work in the campaign," she said curtly.

Oliver was such a boor that he didn't have sense enough to drop the subject. "Must be nice to have friends in high places and land yourself on the governor's task force."

"Listen, Oliver, I got put on the task force because the governor was kind enough to listen to my ideas."

"Sure, sure, but why did he listen to *you?* He didn't ask any of the rest of us what we think." Oliver turned to his friend and gave a knowing smirk.

Meredith tried to hold onto her temper, but the mocking grin on Oliver's face was too much. "I should think the reason he asked *me* and not *you* would be embarrassingly obvious." Her words dripped ice. Before Oliver could recover from his surprise, she turned on her heel and went back to her office.

"Meredith?" inquired the concerned voice of Susan Ortega. "Sorry, but I couldn't help overhearing. You know how voices carry in this office."

Meredith looked up and tried to smile a greeting. "Come on in."

"Look, I don't want to meddle—"

"It's okay. There aren't any secrets around here."

"Meredith, I told you that I've been through this myself. It's really rough when everybody is talking about you behind your back—and to your face, too."

"I didn't realize how bad it was until it happened to me."

Susan smiled sympathetically. "What's that old saying about walking a mile in someone else's moccasins before you judge them?"

"Susan, what am I going to do?"

"I'm glad you asked," Susan responded, sitting down on the vinyl chair usually occupied by a probationer. "You can't afford to make any enemies in this office, Meredith. Oliver doesn't have the sense God gave a turnip, but he's not malicious. Or at least he wasn't. It was just his misguided attempt to be funny. But now you've thrown down the gauntlet, and he'll be watching for you to make a mistake. He'll find things to complain about in your work, or your handling of cases, and the stories will fly faster and faster. In the end, your credit will be gone and you won't be able to function any more."

"It sounds hopeless. I might as well quit and be done with it."

"You can't give up without a fight."

"I don't know how to fight this kind of battle. It's too insidious."

"You can fight it. If you want to."

"How?"

"The same way I did. Keep a low profile. Don't give anybody any reason to find fault. Be cheerful and keep your chin up. And if you can bring yourself to do it, apologize to Oliver."

"*Me* apologize to *him?* Are you kidding?"

"I was afraid you'd say that. But if you could just grit your teeth and do it, I think he would apologize, too. He probably feels pretty bad about what he said. He's not a bad guy, Meredith, just tactless."

Meredith put her head in her hands. "All right," she muttered glumly.

"Well, I've got to get back to work. I have a probationer due any minute." Susan rose to leave Meredith's office.

"Thanks for wanting to help," Meredith said. Their eyes met in understanding.

"Was he worth all this?" Susan said softly as she went out the door. "Judge Baxter, I mean?"

Meredith slowly shook her head. But something in her heart cried yes.

From then on at work Meredith controlled every expression, every word, with an iron-willed discipline. Never had she dressed herself or performed her work with such care. No longer did she wear the bright colors she loved to the office, choosing instead all the most neutral, severe clothes available. She did some shopping, deciding that the emergency justified a liberal use of her charge card. She was grateful for the anonymous-looking beiges and grays she found in the shops and hoped that she would simply fade into the woodwork.

The days were an eternity. The block of time from 8:00 A.M. to 5:00 P.M., which never used to be long enough for everything Meredith wanted to accomplish, became a yawning pit impossible to fill. The self-control she exercised at the office was bought at a tremendous price, and night after night Meredith flopped onto her bed and cried into her pillow until the dawn. Her appearance began to suffer, for dark circles formed under her eyes and she lost so much weight that she became gaunt. Her work also began to suffer, because she was too mentally distraught to be capable of the creative thinking that had previously made her work superior. She longed for a cave where she could escape from prying eyes and heal her wounds, and since that was impossible, she exercised a psychological withdrawal, detaching herself mentally and emotionally, if not physically, from the distressful situation.

Harvey Gilstrap, her boss, who was a much better supervisor than people sometimes realized, watched the change in Meredith and grew alarmed. She had been his best probation officer, a source of great pride, and he observed the slow deterioration in her work. Something had to be done to bring Meredith back to life or it would be only a matter of time before she resigned her job. Even Harvey spent a few sleepless nights, tossing and turning until his wife felt like a ship in a storm tossed by the waves. She gave Harvey an ultimatum: Resolve his problem or move to the sofa. The thought of squashing himself onto their narrow sofa was more than adequate motivation. Harvey found a solution.

"Meredith," he bellowed the next morning. "Come in here and close the door."

"What have I done now, Harvey?" she said, shutting the door. She was too listless to care.

"I'm going to make some staff reassignments." Harvey looked quite pleased with himself, but Meredith didn't notice. She was remembering the shuffle that had brought her to the central office from one of the branch offices six months earlier and changed her whole life, she thought dismally. It was too bad she hadn't been left at the branch. Then she would never have met Warren Baxter and none of this would have happened to her.

Harvey waited expectantly for Meredith to respond, but she just sat there. He summoned all his bluster. "Well, now, Meredith," he began, slapping around a few files on his otherwise empty desk. "Ummm . . . here it is, yes. This is my file on your special project for the governor."

Meredith showed only slight interest. "Yes?"

"Well, damn it, Meredith, this is the governor's special task force on penal reform, and you haven't done a thing."

"Now, Harvey," she replied, growing defensive. "The committee has only met once, and I haven't had time to work up a proposal yet. I still have a full caseload of probationers. Some of them are in this office every single day. Then I go visit their families, their employers, go to the jail and fill out all these probation reports—in triplicate." She paused for breath.

Harvey leaned back in his chair and peered at her

over his half-rim glasses. His dimples worked as he pursed his lips in deep concentration. "Are you telling me that your problem is time?" he asked in a soft, kind voice.

"Yes, Harvey, that's what I'm telling you."

"That's just what I thought." He removed his glasses and leaned across the desk. "That's why we're going to have some staff reassignments."

Harvey rolled his chair back from the desk. "Here," he said, stuffing a folder in her hand. "I'm turning your cases over to someone else for the time being. I want you to move out to the Northeast Branch. They have a vacant office out there since Jim Edwards left, and you can work without all the distractions we have down here. I want you to spend all your time developing a plan to present to the task force. There's a good secretary at the branch—Brenda somebody—and you can use her as much as you need to. Write letters, make phone calls, do whatever you have to do."

Meredith couldn't take in all these changes. "You mean I'm not going to work with probationers?"

"Well, no, not right now. How could you? This is a big chance for the probation office, and I don't want you to blow it. You said you need more time. You've got it. All you need."

Meredith was too puzzled to say a word. She looked down at the file folder with a bright blue tab marked "Operation Task Force."

Harvey stood and shooed Meredith out the door. "Don't you let me down, Meredith Jennings. The reputation of the whole Probation Department is at stake. You do a bang-up job on this and you'll do us all proud. You goof up and I'll—" Harvey tried to think of the worst thing he could do to her. "—I'll assign you the toughest cases that come through this department. . . ." His voice trailed into the empty air. Meredith had gone to clean out her desk. Harvey lowered his bulk back into his chair and beamed in self-satisfaction. Meredith was so mad her eyes were shooting sparks. And Harvey doubted if the Northeast Branch had ever even heard of Judge Baxter.

Luckily the downtown gossip did not often make it to the probation branch offices, so Meredith was able to start her new assignment at the Northeast Branch with no reminders of Warren. At work she was able to discipline her mind to forget him, but when she went home at night, she found her memory as sharp as ever. The thought of his urgent demands still brought an answering fire to her loins. Even alone in her own bed, she would experience an electrifying surge of passion that made her heart pound. His kisses, his warmth . . . how she longed for him.

She often read about him in the newspapers because he had presided over several important trials, and there were regular reports on the local television newscasts as well. Bettis Langley always gave coverage to stories about Warren, and in the newscasts he was as handsome and irresistible as ever. It intrigued Meredith to observe the kind of role Warren played for the television cameras, full of "good ol' boy" charm for the voters. That politician's role, informal and appealing, was very different from his judicial role, austere and disciplined. And both of those roles were totally different from the person Meredith knew, sometimes passionate, sometimes cold. His personality was so many-faceted that she never knew what to expect from him and was always having to adjust to a new dimension.

But no more. She had not heard from him in weeks,

not since the day of the inauguration. He cared nothing for her or he would have at least telephoned. She would not mind having to pretend there was nothing between them when other people were around, if only he would call and let her know that he still . . . *wanted* her. She would settle for that much. Or that little.

She wanted more. She wanted him totally, emotionally as well as physically, but he was incapable of giving himself emotionally. That part of him was safely locked away. Meredith had to face that truth about his character. And she was ashamed of what she knew about herself: it was true—she would settle for the physical if that was all Warren could give. To experience that passion with Warren would be better than to have everything with someone else.

Yet even that was denied her. Warren had changed his mind and there was nothing she could do about it. She had to do something to fill the void in her life, and so she threw herself into her work with the total abandon she would have given to a love affair. The Northeast Branch discovered that Meredith was a dynamo.

Meredith absentmindedly brushed her hair back out of her eyes and continued to dictate a letter while she stood at the secretary's desk.

The Northeast Branch was a small office located over a corner grocery store, with just enough room for a tiny reception area, cubicles for half a dozen probation officers, and an all-purpose room that doubled for conferences and coffee breaks. It had been established to serve probationers who lived in that section of Austin and was organized to make probation visits as convenient as possible. Each probation officer took a turn working late one evening a week so that probationers with jobs could report after work. The branch was usually in a state of organized chaos, with telephones ringing in every office and probationers coming in and out to make their monthly reports. Brenda, the secretary, also performed receptionist duties, so Meredith did not have the luxury of dictating in her own office. She had to stand in the reception area and dictate in between telephone calls. Brenda had enormous powers of concentration, though, so the situation was reasonably tolerable.

"Thanks, Brenda. While you're typing up that letter, I'll go through the mail. It looks like a lot of people are already responding to my telephone requests." Meredith picked up a large bundle of letters and wandered back down the hall to her own office. She had spent two busy months at the Northeast Branch, and things were beginning to shape up at last. She had thought the hardest part of her new assignment would be working out a program that would achieve the kind of rehabilitation she had in mind. To her surprise, she had discovered that the planning was the easy part. The hard part had been to sell the program to the people who counted.

Every day she had dressed in her most professional looking outfits and gone from one local agency to another, trying to enlist support. She had charmed, intimidated, coaxed, argued and pleaded until finally the tide turned and people began to think seriously about her proposal. Some agency heads had reservations, perhaps justified, about the program. After all, it was a new approach, completely untried, and there was no way to know whether it would work. Meredith had listened carefully to the suggestions of the people who would be working with her and modified the plan until she thought she had ironed out all the problem areas.

She would soon find out, and she felt the flutter of butterflies in her stomach as she thought of the unveiling to come.

She unfolded another letter, this one from the Deaf Citizens Program. Wonderful. They wanted to get in on the act, too, and would be sending a representative to this afternoon's meeting. Meredith walked over to the conference room and counted the chairs. She hoped there would be enough for everybody. She placed the bulging file folder with its tattered blue tab marked "Operation Task Force" on the corner of the conference table and said a silent prayer that all would go well at the meeting. Then she left to treat Brenda to a well-earned lunch at the Old Pecan Street Cafe.

The probation office coffee definitely didn't compare with the freshly ground Colombian at the Old Pecan Street Cafe, Meredith thought, stirring the black syrup in her Styrofoam cup. The conference room was crowded with visitors, all chit-chatting while they waited for the meeting to start. Harvey sat back in the corner with his hands folded across his ample stomach and waited expectantly. Meredith swallowed hard as she remembered his threat to assign her all the most difficult cases if she goofed up on this project. Promptly at three o'clock she asked everyone to be seated, and the meeting began.

"I've talked to all of you at least once, and some of you many times, about the new probation program we want to implement on a trial basis. We think it has lots of potential, but it won't work unless we get your cooperation. If we're successful, we'll not only help the probationers, we will see a great return for the community. Let me tell you how it's going to work," she said, placing a large poster on an easel and explaining its significance.

The questions came quickly and were to the point. "Are we going to have to be responsible for the probationers? Isn't that *your* job?"

"Oh, yes. It will still be the job of the probation officer to supervise the defendants," Meredith answered. "We ask you to let the defendant come to you for a definite number of hours each week and do the work you assign to him. You will only supervise his performance on that particular task. If it isn't satisfactory, you tell me and I'll handle it from there."

"What if the defendant is lazy or surly and won't do the work?" questioned someone else.

"We're going to select only people with the greatest chance of success for this pilot program. We hope you'll have highly motivated people to work with. After all, if they make you happy, they can keep themselves out of prison. But we may make a mistake. Someone may not work out. That's why we'll assign only people convicted of minor crimes, such as writing hot checks or driving while intoxicated. That way, if we guess wrong about someone's potential and motivation, the community is assuming comparatively slight risk of harm."

"How are we going to pay these people? Our budget is strapped as it is," asked a money-conscious administrator from the county hospital.

"Their work will be done on a volunteer basis. They will receive no salary whatsoever. Their work for the community is part of their fine, except instead of a money fine, they'll be assessed a certain number of hours to work. It's part of their restitution to the city. That's why we're calling our pilot program 'CSR,' or 'Community Service Restitution.' " The thought of free labor brought smiles to most of the faces. These were administrators from various local agencies, all of them only too familiar with limited budgets and expanding responsibilities. Their enthusiasm for the project began to grow.

By five o'clock Meredith had won their approval. Twenty agencies agreed to serve as sponsors, each accepting five defendants for a period of six months. At the end of that time the program would be evaluated and a decision would be made regarding continuance of the project.

Meredith was thrilled with their response. She expressed her appreciation for their willingness to be part of a pilot program and reminded them that the cost of keeping someone in prison came to five times the cost of probation. If they could work together to make the CSR program a success, everybody would come out ahead, including the taxpayers.

The meeting broke up and the visitors left, giving Meredith their good wishes for the project. She sank into a chair and kicked off her shoes while Harvey poured himself another cup of coffee and settled back for a chat.

Meredith had worked unstintingly for two months, and today Harvey saw that her labors had paid off; she had come a long way since he transferred her. She had thrown herself into the assignment with all her energy and ingenuity, and he was proud of the result.

Meredith, too, was pleased with the response to her new proposal. It helped to fill the emptiness left by Warren's departure from her life. She wondered whether she would ever be able to forget Warren and decided no amount of activity would take his place. Still, she was glad Harvey had given her an absorbing project to work on. If she were still involved in the daily routine of a probation officer's job, she would have found it impossible to put Warren out of her mind for any part of the day. There were still too many times when she would remember his voice, the laughter in his eyes, his tall, tanned body, and feel a white heat that drove her to torment. Those memories kept her desire aflame even though she knew it would never be gratified.

"You've done a fine job, Meredith," Harvey said with sincerity. "I believe you've sold it to these folks, anyhow."

"This is just the beginning, Harvey. Once we find out whether it will work—and it *will* work, it has to—then we can start expanding. Why, I bet we can eventually put all our minor offenders on CSR. Don't you think so?"

Harvey looked into Meredith's happy face and smiled. "If we get the breaks, gal, if we get the breaks."

Meredith twirled circles with her stockinged foot. "I'm tired, Harvey. I think I'll go home and dig in my azaleas for a while and see if I can unwind. They ought to be blooming pretty soon, if it stays warm."

"Let me talk to you about one more thing before you go," Harvey said, leaning back his head and gazing innocently at the ceiling. His chubby knuckles drummed against his belt buckle.

Meredith was on guard immediately. Harvey had not outmaneuvered her for a long time, but she knew the signs. She forgot about her azaleas. "Harvey . . . " she said, her voice rising.

"Just a gol-dern minute, before you get yourself all fired up," he said, waving his hand impatiently. "You've been so busy getting ready for this meeting that I haven't had time to talk to you—"

"About what?" Meredith interrupted.

"A seminar for probation officers over in San Antonio next week. I want you to go."

"Is that all?" Meredith breathed a sigh of relief. Seminars were all part of a day's work. Sometimes they were worthwhile and helped her do a better job.

"Not exactly." Harvey scooted his chair out of harm's way. He didn't like the look Meredith was giving him. "They asked Travis County to furnish a speaker for one of the workshops."

"So?"

"So I turned in your name."

"You what?" Meredith's voice went up an octave.

"Now, Meredith, there's nothing to it." Harvey's voice dripped honey. "All you have to do is give the same little talk you gave to the folks here today. You can even use the same chart and everything."

"You mean you expect me to get up in front of a group of strangers and tell them about a brand-new program when we don't even know if it's going to work? Harvey, have you lost your mind?"

"Now, Meredith, the governor had enough confidence in you to put you on the state task force. I've got just as much confidence in you as he does. You're the best probation officer I've got," he said.

"Okay, okay," she muttered, knowing it was a losing battle when Harvey made up his mind.

"That's a good girl," he beamed. "I knew you'd come around." He reached in a folder and pulled out a printed bulletin. "Here you are. This tells all about the seminar. See, here's your name printed right here for Workshop VI, 'Innovative Approaches to Probation Utilizing Community Resources.'"

"Harvey Gilstrap, do you mean to say that you committed me to do this without even asking and they've already printed my name on this thing?" The sound that came from her throat could only be described as a growl. Harvey propelled himself out of the chair and headed toward the door.

Meredith sank into a chair and looked at the bulletin in disgust. Harvey had about as much sense as a retarded duck. She flipped the pages of the bulletin to see who else would be there. A soft gasp escaped her throat. In large letters she read, "KEYNOTE SPEAKER: HONORABLE WARREN BAXTER, District Judge of Travis County."

Chapter Eight

Meredith's battered Volkswagen pulled into a parking space near the Hilton Palacio del Rio in San Antonio promptly at nine o'clock the next Friday morning. She had allowed herself an extra thirty minutes to find the seminar location and set up the materials she carried in her well-traveled briefcase. She glanced into the rearview mirror and smoothed a strand of blonde hair back into the roped coil at the base of her neck, then let out her breath in a nervous sigh and stepped out of the car.

She had been in a dither all week, excited about the

chance to share her ideas with other cities and jittery about seeing Warren. This was to be a small seminar with fewer than 75 participants, so it was inevitable that they would meet. He had hardly spoken to her since the inauguration in January. She had felt alternately hurt, confused, depressed, angry and bitter during these long weeks, but finally she had achieved a kind of resignation—until she found out they would be attending the same seminar. Now she didn't know what she felt. There was a crazy racing in her veins, and she had spent more time during the week worrying about what to wear than about what to say in her presentation.

Instead of wearing one of the easily forgettable grays she had recently bought, Meredith had indulged in a fit of reckless extravagance and bought a new textured silk suit. Its tailored blazer was pin-striped in coffee-and-cream, and its dirndl skirt was solid-colored coffee. She wore a cream-colored blouse with a soft bow at the neck, and with her hair coiled back she looked businesslike, yet totally feminine. She wished she felt as composed as she looked and hoped the total effect was worth two weeks' salary. Butterflies were doing a polka in her stomach.

The clerk at the Information Desk looked up in genuine admiration as Meredith walked through the carved wooden doors, her high-heeled lizard pumps clicking against the terra-cotta tile. He personally escorted her through the lobby, decorated in the historic Spanish period, to the La Vista Room where the keynote address would be given. There she found other early arrivals sipping strong Mexican coffee and munching warm buttered tortillas. She smiled and signed her name at the registration table, surreptitiously scanning the room for Warren. He was nowhere to be seen, but there were other probation officers from various parts of the state whom she had met at previous seminars. The other participants were mostly fat, balding males in discount-store sportcoats, and they converged on her, eager to be in the presence of a beautiful woman. Meredith smiled, enjoying the attention, and decided her new suit was worth every cent.

She chatted briefly with them and then excused herself to set up her materials in the room where her workshop would be conducted at 4:00 P.M. She had been disappointed to be assigned such a late hour because she knew that inevitably most of the participants would begin slipping away from the meeting by late afternoon. The ones who remained would be tired and bored, and it would be difficult to generate any enthusiasm for her project. But those were factors outside her control. All she could do was to give it her best effort and hope to spark some kind of interest. She arranged her materials in neat stacks on a table and realized she had probably been overly optimistic when she had asked Brenda to run off fifty copies of everything. She would be lucky to have six people present. Oh, well, *c'est la vie.*

Meredith returned to the large meeting room and ran smack into Warren Baxter, accompanied by the Director of the State Criminal Justice Division. Warren shook hands very properly and made the introductions. The whole situation seemed a charade that Meredith watched from outside herself. She turned to the other man, extended her hand, smiled, and conversed, as if in a dream. Yet all the time her attention was focused on Warren and his on her. She noticed a drawn look about his dark eyes, though the same gold flecks hinted at lazy fires within. She quickly averted her glance, but she could not hide the telltale blush of excitement at seeing him again. With a shaky smile, she turned to the director, who promptly insisted that she join their group for lunch at the end of the morning session.

Warren, who had spent the week wondering how he would react to seeing Meredith again after all this time, found that his passion had only been dormant, not dead, and was rekindled in an instant. He had anticipated that might happen, though, and had determined that no matter how strong his feelings might become, he would keep them under control. He had no intention of letting anything happen that might compromise them or generate any further gossip. Still, there was nothing wrong with a social conversation. As other people joined their group, Warren found a moment for a brief aside.

"How have you been?" he asked. "You look thin." His eyes searched her with concern.

Meredith had forgotten that she had lost weight. Warren had not seen her for at least two months. "I'm fine, just working hard. How about you?"

"Oh, the same." No need to mention that life had taken on a dull monotony without her presence. Or that he had counted the hours until this seminar. He fingered the nick on his chin where he had cut himself shaving this morning. He hadn't done that since he was in high school, but today his fingers had been too unsteady to hold the razor.

There was an awkward pause. There was nothing to say and at the same time everything to say. Their eyes met in a question for which there was no answer. Then Warren was dragged away to the podium by the administrative assistant who was in charge of arrangements. Meredith excused herself from the remaining group and went to the ladies' restroom, her hands shaking and her eyes brilliant. She splashed cold water on her face and carefully blotted it so that she would not disturb her makeup. Then she leaned against the tiled wall and tried to steel herself for the day.

Years of practicing law had made Warren an effective public speaker. Meredith was surprised at the persona he assumed in front of a crowd—folksy and homespun, very different from the intimidating arrogance he was capable of in his courtroom. It was yet another side to his personality, and Meredith realized that she really didn't know Warren at all. She knew only certain aspects of what must assuredly be a very complex person. Wondering if she would ever really know him, or if anybody else could, she grew thoughtful.

Warren warmed up his audience by beginning his speech with several amusing and well-told jokes before he outlined the broad range of the criminal justice program and its general objectives. Reminding his listeners that there were many agencies with overlapping responsibilities, he noted that an effective program required full cooperation from everybody. He then focused specifically on the tension between the courts and the probation office.

"I know some of you are wondering why I was chosen to speak at this seminar. Why, some of you call me 'Old Lock 'em Up and Leave 'em.'" There were guffaws of laughter. "I do have a reputation for being a tough judge, and some of you are sorry when your defendants wind up in my court." Meredith fixed her eyes on her hands in her lap, but she could feel Warren's gaze prodding her. She kept her head down.

"However, you and I have to work together if the

system is going to work," he continued. "I'm going to tell you a story I've told only one person before." Meredith tensed. What was he going to tell them? "It's pretty personal, and I'm not very proud of it. As a matter of fact, I'd rather not think about it. But I'm going to tell it to you this morning as a reminder to all of us that we have to keep our heads screwed on straight if we're going to do the job the public has entrusted to us." By this time the audience were on the edge of their seats, wondering what revelation was about to be made. Warren told his story with maximum effect—the same story he had earlier told Meredith about the oil field worker whom he had helped to get probation, only to have the defendant go back to Arkansas and beat his wife to death. When he finished the story there was a hushed silence in the room. Visibly shaken, Warren cleared his throat while tension hung in the air. He didn't continue for several moments. "That incident has haunted me for all these years," he said at last. "Maybe I've lost my sense of proportion and see that oil field worker inside every defendant who stands before me, so I don't trust any of them."

Meredith was bewildered. Where was he headed? She didn't know what to expect next.

Warren gripped the podium and spoke softly into the microphone. "Lately I've come to realize that there can't be any 'justice' in the system if each individual defendant isn't judged on his own merits. It's too simplistic to send everybody to prison for fear some defendants won't live up to probation conditions. I urge you to find ways to help judges know which defendants can be trusted. Get us the information that will make a difference. Talk to their families, friends, employers, teachers, psychologists, doctors—talk to anybody who knows. We need your help. We can't do it ourselves. We're in the courtroom. We have to depend on you. But if you'll do that and get us enough information to make a rational decision, maybe we can prevent our state's personal and financial resources from going down the drain. Thank you."

Warren sat down to hearty applause. In the row in front of Meredith someone stood, and then another, and soon they were all on their feet, giving Warren a stirring standing ovation. He stood, head bowed, at a loss for words. The director, standing next to Warren at the podium, turned and clapped him on the back, and then the crowd surged forward to shake his hand.

Meredith hung back, not knowing how to react. She was stunned. The Warren she thought she knew would never have made a public confession of doubt or asked for help from other people. Certainly he would never have admitted that he might be wrong. What had happened to him in the past few months? She watched him from the sidelines but found no explanation. He seemed to have recovered and welcomed the probation officers with hearty handshakes. Tall, rugged, easily the most attractive man in the room in a well-tailored suit, he radiated confidence and energy. Meredith went to the back of the room to get a cup of coffee and escape from the situation. She could not shake Warren's hand. She would not know what to say to him.

The room was in disorder, but since a coffee break was scheduled next, it really didn't matter. Admirers thronged about him, eager for a personal word and touch. Meredith was accustomed to seeing Warren in a different environment and was surprised at the charismatic effect he had on the crowd. She had always been aware of his dynamic energy, but in the formal situation of the courtroom or his office, his teeming magnetism was well-controlled. In this crowd, it was turned loose, and she realized that his leadership exuded the kind of confidence that inspired people to follow him, made them *eager* to follow him. She studied the crowd swarming around him and smiled. No wonder Warren had been elected judge so easily.

After twenty minutes of hubbub, the audience was called to order for the next speaker. Meredith took an empty seat at the rear of the room and was surprised when a warm arm gripped her shoulder. Warren had taken the seat next to her. The group's reaction to his speech and the catharsis of expressing doubts about an old mistake had stirred him. He was hard-pressed to curb the excitement that flowed through his lean body.

"Where were you?" he whispered. "I shook every hand in this room except yours." Flecks of gold danced in his dark eyes.

"Sorry," she answered, hastily offering her hand. She made the gesture in jest but immediately knew she had made a disastrous mistake. Warmth from his hand spread up her arm with a languid fire. She jerked her hand free and turned back to the speaker. Warren grinned and squirmed into a more comfortable position, casually draping his arm across the back of her chair. His fingers toyed with the back of her collar. "Please, don't," she implored him. She had no idea what the speaker was saying. Her notebook lay abandoned in her lap.

Warren's fingers moved to the hair coiled at the nape of her neck. Shivers shot down her spine. "What have you done to your hair?" he murmured. "I like it." The stimulation from being well-received by the seminar crowd was affecting his good intentions. The desire that he had resolved to stifle seemed to have a will of its own.

"Sssh," she said, scooting her chair away. She picked up the notebook and attempted to jot down the idea the speaker was discussing. But she couldn't hear a word he was saying over the roar in her ears. She fanned her face with the notebook.

"Is something wrong?" Warren whispered. "Your cheeks are burning. Do you have a fever?"

"No," she hissed. "Please be quiet." People nearby turned to stare. Warren grinned and nodded his head to them. They grinned and nodded in return, then tactfully turned their attention back to the speaker. After that Warren behaved himself, concentrating self-consciously on the words booming through the loudspeaker. He took meticulous notes and nodded gravely as the speaker pounded the podium to emphasize a point. Meredith looked down at the doodles scrawled in her notebook—a chain of interlocking hearts—and quickly turned the page. She glanced at Warren out of the corner of her eye, hoping that he had not seen. He seemed to be absorbed in his own notes, thank heavens. Or so she thought, until she glanced at them and saw a chain of interlocking arrows in the margin. She dropped her pen as if it were the guilty party and wiggled in her chair, looking at her watch to see how much time remained. This was the longest speech she had ever attended. She stared straight ahead and concentrated on surviving.

A smattering of applause brought her back to the present. There was a shuffling of chairs and people stood to stretch. They were on their own for lunch, with the meeting to reconvene in an hour. She reached for her lizard bag, ready to bolt the room, but the director hurried toward her. "Meredith, let me round up the others and we'll all catch a bite somewhere nearby."

"Excuse me," Meredith said brightly to Warren. She needed to get away from him and was glad to have the lunch invitation. Her relief was short-lived however.

"No need to rush away," Warren said. "I'm invited, too." Without waiting for her response, he took her arm and guided her across the room to the group of colleagues gathered up by the director. There were seven of them, surely enough to provide plenty of distraction. Meredith hoped she would be safe in the crowd.

They left the Hilton and went outside, looking up and down the busy street trying to decide which restaurant would be fast and good. The sky was still as overcast as it had been when Meredith drove the ninety miles from Austin this morning, and the gray clouds did nothing to improve her mood. She thought she would scream with frustration while the group tried to decide where to eat. How can seven adults spend so much time doing nothing? she wondered. Nobody wanted to make a choice among the various suggestions. What possible difference did it make? In her present state of nerves, the food was going to taste like stewed cardboard anyway. She seized upon one of the proposals. "How about the chili parlor?" she asked.

It probably didn't take any longer than five minutes for them to discuss the fact that none of them had ever eaten there before and consider whether they were brave enough to go to an untried restaurant. Invigorated by the morning's speeches, though, they took the risk. They trooped two blocks over to Commerce Street for the culinary adventure of spicy, Texas-style chili. Meredith took a seat at the end of a bench with room for only one person, and Warren seated himself across from her. He studiously ignored her and set himself to entertaining the group, telling witty stories about unusual happenings on the bench.

It was impossible however, to ignore the hot chili, and Meredith found herself having to wash it down with huge quantities of iced tea. Half of the Texas-sized portion was all she could eat, though the men in the group were able to polish off their entire serving, well laced with hot pepper sauce. Meredith suspected they would sweat all afternoon, but the peppers should keep them awake for the rest of the seminar.

Meredith joined in the bantering conversation and felt herself unwind. Everybody had "war stories" about their on-the-job perils and antics. One man talked about the old days when there were no female probation officers and he had to finagle his way out of the compromising situations he got into trying to supervise female defendants. The irate husband of one defendant had threatened to fill his britches with buckshot on the mistaken assumption that he was a Casanova with designs on his wife. He turned to Meredith with a broad grin and said he was all for progress, especially when the female probation officers turned out to be as pretty, and as smart, as she was. There was a general chorus of agreement, and Meredith quickly changed the subject to baseball—and the good fortune the Texas Rangers had with their recent trades.

While the conversation hummed around her, she looked out the window at the tourists going past and realized that there were not many "locals" in this part of San Antonio. This was such a beautiful area of the city, near the San Antonio River and the old Hemisfair, that it was tailor-made for the tourist industry. Spring had brought the trees and vegetation to a bright, verdant green and there were already shrubs flowering everywhere. It could be such a romantic place, she thought wistfully, glancing at Warren, who was preoccupied with telling a hilarious anecdote. She still could not adjust to the change in his personality since he was away from his court. He finished his story to peals of laughter, then looked at his watch and suggested that it was time for them to go back to the Hilton.

They strolled back in a noisy, jovial group, swapping insults and peering in store windows. Warren took Meredith's arm to cross the street and they had their first private conversation.

"Why don't you have dinner with me after the seminar is over?" he asked. He had decided that a casual dinner would be perfectly safe. A nice meal, a couple of hours' conversation, and then back to Austin, with no one the wiser. Once the seminar participants scattered, there would be no one in San Antonio who knew either of them. Surely they were entitled to that much.

Meredith looked up into his eager eyes and started to shake her head.

"Aw, come on. Have you ever eaten good Mexican food out on the river?"

Meredith dropped her eyes. "Well, no."

"I promise you, you'll love it. Nothing like it anywhere else."

She was undecided. Dinner seemed harmless enough. The light changed to green and they went across the street.

"It's Friday, so it won't hurt to stay a couple of extra hours. You don't have to work tomorrow." Though his words were coaxing, his tone was nonchalant, as though it really didn't matter to him one way or the other. "Last chance," he said with a grin as they entered the hotel lobby. "If you say no, I'll ask Merdine Shinabarger."

Meredith laughed. "In that case, the answer is yes," she answered. "Anything to save you from Merdine."

The afternoon flew past. Meredith attended two workshops presented by other probation officers and then at four o'clock made her own presentation. To her surprise, most of the participants remained for the conclusion of the seminar, and there were thirty-five people in her group. They came from all over the state, big towns and small, all the way from Amarillo in the Panhandle to Beaumont near the Gulf. She was excited to think that her ideas would have a chance to spread so far. Some of the people were skeptical, although everybody seemed interested. They asked for updates when the Austin evaluation was completed in six months, and one eager young probation officer from Lampasas wanted to get started right away. Meredith's materials quickly disappeared when she offered them to the group, and she was glad after all that she had asked Brenda to run off fifty copies, since some people wanted extras to take back to their colleagues. As much as their interest, Meredith appreciated their good will, for all of them wanted to see a fellow probation officer advance, and they congratulated her sincerely for her creative ideas. The workshop ended on a positive note, and Meredith went in a state of euphoria to find Warren.

She found him leaning against a doorpost smoking a cigarette. "How did it go?" he asked.

"Pretty well." She gave him a dazzling smile.

"I thought so. Your eyes are dancing."

She blushed. "I got a kick out of doing it."

"Sure you did. You got some well-deserved recognition. That will put sparkles in anybody's eyes." He grinned at her and gave her the casual but affectionate hug of a brother. "Are you ready for the world's best Mexican food?"

"You bet. Lead me to it."

They walked through the Hilton and emerged on the side facing the river. The city was hauntingly beautiful, and they strolled the riverwalk with the scent of flowers hanging in the air. The riverwalk was lined with bars and cafes for the *touristas,* and as they walked past they heard snatches of music coming from inside. Irish folksongs in one club were followed by New Orleans jazz in another, and from somewhere farther away they could hear the pulsating bass of a rock band. Tourists struggled to adjust their cameras for the gray haze of the sky, reflected now in the river. They walked over a stone bridge and entered Casa Rio.

"Would you like a drink first?" Warren asked.

"If you would."

"It's Friday night. Why not? The margaritas are superb." He motioned to the barmaid and ordered two drinks which appeared very promptly. Warren, ruggedly handsome in a dark suit with crisp white shirt and burgundy tie, merited special attention.

They slowly sipped their pale green drinks, which were everything Warren had promised—the perfect combination of tartness and sweetness. Warren was careful in his behavior toward Meredith, almost as if he were afraid that if he pressed any kind of attentions on her, she would run away. He was warm and friendly, but anybody who watched them together would think theirs was an old, casual friendship from school days.

He knew that being together would ignite the passion that lurked just beneath the surface unless they shielded themselves. He wanted them to have this brief, precious time together, but not at the risk of unleashing torrents of desire. He willed himself to be cordial, nothing more. There was a certain affection in his smile and in the way he sometimes touched her wrist as they talked, but nothing that would set up her guard or make her tense. She relaxed, perhaps for the first time ever with Warren, and felt entirely comfortable simply getting to know him better. If occasionally her eyes lingered on the laugh lines at his eyes or the way his dark hair cupped his ear, Meredith was unaware of it.

A mariachi band approached their table and sang a sad, romantic ballad in Spanish, madly thumping their guitars at its tragic conclusion. The lead guitarist used his snapping black eyes and brilliant white teeth to flirt outrageously with Meredith, and it took a large tip and a firm "no" from Warren to send them on their way. The tequila had already begun to reach Meredith's bloodstream, and she giggled, pleased at their attentions.

"I think we need to get you some food before you get tipsy," Warren said, smiling. "These margaritas are dynamite."

Meredith finished her last sip. "Let's have one more—a small one this time," she said.

"We have to drive back to Austin, Meredith. Sure you'll be all right?"

"Oh, sure. Dinner should take care of the alcohol and if it doesn't, I'll have some strong coffee with dessert."

Warren shrugged. "If you say so," he said, summoning the barmaid. "Can you bring us some *tostadas* and *salsa* to go with our drinks?" he requested. The barmaid's answering smile assured Warren that she was happy to oblige him.

"Wow!" Meredith said. "I think you've made a conquest!"

"Well, no more than your damned mariachi player," Warren answered.

Meredith raised a slim finger and sliced the air. "One for you," she said.

"One-up," he answered.

They took their fresh drinks out on the riverwalk and breathed in the sea breeze. "It almost smells like rain," Meredith said, glancing up into the haze. She smoothed her hair back into its coil. There were some loose strands that felt like they were beginning to frizz.

There were barges out on the river, some docked and some gliding slowly into the distance. "Would you like to eat dinner out on the river?" Warren asked. "The restaurant has a boat for guests who want to enjoy a leisurely ride in the water while they dine."

"Oh, could we?" Meredith was delighted. "I've never seen that done anywhere. It sounds like fun."

"Let's go turn in our order and the waiter will serve us on the boat."

Meredith eagerly followed Warren back into the restaurant, where he consulted with the maître d' and then brought a menu for Meredith to study. "The enchiladas sound good," she said.

"Too ordinary. Don't you want to try something different?"

"Hummm." She wrinkled her brow in concentration. "What about the *menudo?* I've never had that before."

"Ahh. Do you like *tripes?"*

She translated the Spanish word. T-r-i-p-e. Tripe! "Intestines?" she said, horrified.

Warren nodded. "Maybe you'd like something else?"

"Definitely."

"The *chile rellenos* are good," he suggested. "They're different from the ones in Austin. They're made of *poblano* peppers stuffed with *picadillo.*"

"What's that?"

"Beef and raisins. And the *chile con queso* poured on the top is fantastic."

"Oh, definitely the *chile rellenos* then." It sounded bizarre, but it was better than tripe. What did Warren have against enchiladas?

Warren placed their order and they wandered back outside the restaurant to wait for their boat. Meredith's knees were beginning to feel a little trembly from the tequila, so she headed for a bench adjacent to the riverwalk and sank onto it.

"How's your drink?" he asked, noticing that her stemmed glass was nearly empty.

"Delicious. Best margarita I've ever had." She stretched out her arm and handed him her glass.

"No more," he said, quite firmly. "I don't want to be responsible for your having a wreck on the way home tonight."

"It's only ninety miles."

"Meredith, you know I'm a stick-in-the-mud when it comes to mixing driving and drinking." It was a pointed reference to the night he had driven Scott home from the Fall Drunk. She hastily changed the subject. It wouldn't do for either one of them to remember her belly dance that Halloween night.

When the Casa Rio boat docked, Warren helped Meredith aboard. Though they were joined by a few other passengers, they were seated at a corner table where there was relative privacy.

A cheerful Mexican waiter served their meal on a

crisp white tablecloth and lit a candle in a latticed tin lamp that cast a flickering shadow. Dusk was beginning to fall, earlier than usual because of the heavy cloud cover, and all up and down the riverwalk small bright lights began to twinkle. Their table was one of ten on a large, flat-bottomed boat protected with a rail that ran around the sides and piloted by a handsome dark-skinned youth who operated the motor at the rear of the boat. Another Mexican man, darkly handsome, slowly toured the boat with his guitar, singing a medley of romantic ballads in a deep, rich baritone. The boat moved lazily down the river, occasionally encountering other boats carrying a similar load of *touristas* enjoying the lush foliage and the sparkling, shimmering lights reflected on the water.

Their *chile rellenos* were served on piping hot plates that required the use of pot holders. Their waiter brought a straw basket of hot tostadas to dip in guacamole or *salsa* and another basket of warm tortillas to spread with butter. There were small dishes of refried beans and Spanish rice, and for dessert the waiter brought hot, puffy *sopapillas* to break apart and fill with butter and honey. He also insisted that they try the fried ice cream.

Several steaming cups of rich, dark Mexican coffee diluted the alcohol in Meredith's bloodstream, although she still felt a little light-headed. Meredith and Warren were content to eat in a comfortable silence broken only by comments on the delicious food. Meredith thought it was entirely possible that this was the most delicious meal she had ever eaten. She leaned back in her chair and smiled at the sight of Warren wolfing down the last few bites of the guacamole. She sighed with pleasure.

"Now aren't you glad you came?" Warren teased.

"Oh, I am. I wouldn't have missed this meal for the world."

"Meal?" he said, pretending to be offended. "What about the caliber of the company?"

Meredith's tinkling laugh echoed over the lapping waves of the river. "Now, really, you were so busy enjoying your dinner that you didn't even notice I was here."

For just a second there was a flash of fire in Warren's eyes. Softly he murmured, "It wouldn't take long to prove you wrong about that." Meredith's eyes fell to the table and she toyed with the remnants of a *sopapilla.* She hoped her blush would not show in the dim glow of the candle.

Warren studied her face for a long moment. He patted her hand and changed the subject. "There's the Hilton just ahead." Meredith turned to see that the lights had been turned on and they twinkled in the trees in front of the hotel. It was a fairy-tale setting. She sighed. It had been such a wonderful evening and now it was over.

Warren's generous tip assured them of eager assistance as they disembarked at the Casa Rio where their boat ride had begun. "You should hurry, *señor,*" the pilot advised, with a smile that showed perfect white teeth. "This is our last trip for the evening. The Weather Bureau she says we get a storm."

"Thank you, Carlos," Warren said, taking Meredith's hand and pulling her onto the dock. They glanced at the sky, which did seem to have become darker in the past few minutes. But it was after nine o'clock and not unusually dark for the hour. They strolled back toward the hotel, lingering to enjoy the fading moments of a perfect day. They looked in all the shop windows, and when Meredith admired a crystal paperweight embedded with a beautiful, coral-colored seashell, Warren went inside and bought it for her.

"All *touristas* must have a souvenir," he said, placing it in her hand.

"Thank you," she whispered. "I'll keep it to remind me of this lovely evening."

A ragtime piano from a nearby club pounded out a lively tune, and Warren took Meredith's arm and whirled her in a brief, spontaneous soft-shoe. Breathless, they collapsed against a stone building, laughing. "I think you're better at the waltz," Meredith said.

"I think you're better at the belly dance," he retorted.

It was too late to be embarrassed. "I don't believe you'll ever let me live that down," she said, able now to laugh at herself.

"I should think not. I fully expect you to do it again for me some day." There was a dare in his voice, just enough to sound dangerous.

"We'll see," Meredith replied, as lightly as she could.

They stepped away from the building to continue down the street at the exact moment a bolt of lightning split the sky. They looked toward the sky and the first large drops of rain splashed in their faces.

"Hurry, Warren," Meredith said, lengthening her steps. He took her hand and they ran around the side of the building to the Hilton parking lot. "There's my car right over there," she cried, running while raindrops pelted their backs. They jumped in the Volkswagen and waited for the rain to stop.

Chapter Nine

The scattered raindrops quickly turned into sheets of rain that pounded against Meredith's long-suffering Volkswagen.

"Good grief," Meredith exclaimed. "We made it in the nick of time." She moved a little farther away from the door to dodge water leaking in around the window. Being inside the Volkswagen was like being inside a tiny submarine. It was too dark to see anything, and their world seemed to be seaborne, pummeled by waves of water. Lightning bolts flashed, followed by angry claps of thunder.

Meredith became aware of the dampness in her

clothing. The temperature had dropped as suddenly as the cold front arrived, and her teeth began to chatter.

"Take off your jacket," Warren suggested, struggling in the small interior to pull his long arms out of his suitcoat. "You won't feel so cold. The dampness cuts through like a knife." He helped Meredith, then placed their jackets on the back seat to keep them from wrinkling. She could not see Warren, but Meredith was acutely aware of his soft breathing, the warmth radiating from his body in the other bucket seat. All his animal energy was confined to the narrow limits of the Volkswagen, and its magnetic force seemed to multiply in inverse proportion to its concentrated area. She decided she would be safer if she put her mind on the terrors of the thunderstorm.

"This isn't even weather for ducks," Warren complained.

"Ducks? Whales would have a hard time in this storm!"

"I don't believe you can compare this Volkswagen to a whale. Jonah was probably more comfortable than we are."

Meredith tried to examine the shape in the darkness beside her and realized that Warren's legs were too long for the space so that his knees were hunched up around his neck.

"You can move the seat back," she suggested helpfully.

"It *is* back."

"Oh." She tried to think. "Are you terribly uncomfortable?"

"Oh, no. It's perfect."

"Do I detect a note of irony in your voice?"

He laughed and did not answer.

Meredith reached for the radio dial. "I'll play some

music for you so you can relax. I wouldn't want you to get cramped muscles."

"Are you sure the radio won't run down the battery?"

"Are you making fun of my car?" She tuned the dial until she picked up a San Antonio station. Soft music filled the car but did not block out the noise from the roaring thunder.

"Why don't you see if you can find a classic-music station?" Warren said wryly. "Maybe they're playing Tchaikovsky's *1812 Overture.* That would be more appropriate for this storm."

The song ended, and the deejay immediately captured their attention with a weather bulletin: "The National Weather Service reports that flash flood warnings for Central Texas will remain in effect until 3:00 A.M. Creeks are over their banks in Guadalupe and Hays Counties, and there are reports of flooding as far away as Austin. The San Antonio River is rising and residents are urged to remain in their homes due to high water in some streets. Abandoned cars throughout the county are creating hazardous traffic problems for the sheriff's department and local police. We repeat, flash flood warnings remain in effect until 3:00 A.M. Stay tuned for further weather bulletins."

"Oh, no!" Meredith wailed. The sound of music again filled the car.

"I don't know about you, but I'm not too excited about sitting in this car until 3:00 A.M.," Warren muttered.

"What are we going to do?"

"I think we better go inside and wait in the lobby."

"I suppose you're right."

"Do you have an umbrella anywhere?"

"No. But there's an old blanket on the floor of the back seat."

"That'll have to do." Warren squirmed in the seat and fumbled until his fingers found the blanket. "Here, wrap this around you."

"That's not fair," she protested. "We can both wrap up in it."

"Meredith, that would be like running a three-legged race in this rain. Come on," he ordered impatiently, attempting to drape the blanket around her.

"No. Not unless you do."

"I had forgotten how stubborn you can be." Warren pondered the situation. "Okay," he said. "Take off your shoes so you won't ruin them." He leaned down and untied his own shoes and removed them, then unfolded the blanket to its full length and draped it over his head and down his shoulders. He took his shoes in one hand and checked to be sure that Meredith was ready. She had her shoes in one hand and her bag in the other. "Ready? You wait here and I'll come around and get you."

He pushed open the car door and lunged into rain so heavy it almost knocked him off his feet. He ran around to Meredith's side, where she had already opened the car door and waited for him. She scrambled out of the car and he stretched out his arms and drew her against him. He took a second to be sure she was covered with the blanket, then started down the street with Meredith gasping to keep up with his long steps. "I told you this wasn't going to work," he shouted. He stopped short, caught Meredith into his arms and ran, carrying her, the blanket enshrouding them like a cocoon.

Before they had gone fifty feet the rain had soaked through the blanket and ran in rivulets down their faces. They burst into the doors of the hotel and Warren, breathless from exertion, set Meredith down on her feet. It had all happened so fast there was no time to think, but Meredith's heart still hammered from the excitement of being held so close and feeling so protected. Warren shook out the blanket and attempted, without much success, to refold the soggy mess it had become. He wiped the rainwater out of his eyes and ran his fingers through his drenched hair.

The doorman, surprised that anybody would be out in such a storm, hurried from the desk where he had been drinking coffee with the night clerk. "Can I help you, sir?" he asked. Even soaked, Warren was obviously someone of importance.

"I think we're going to have to get a room so we can dry off. Can the valet do something about getting our clothes dry?"

"I'll check, sir." The doorman was well-trained. There was not even a flicker of doubt in his expression.

The lobby was deserted except for the hotel employees. Meredith was grateful there was nobody to witness their bedraggled appearance—or her confusion. Her heart was still doing crazy things. And she was being swept along by the force of Warren's decisions. What would she say if he asked her opinion about taking a hotel room? she wondered. And did she really have any other choice?

Warren walked briskly to the desk, every inch a judge, even in his stocking feet. She heard him murmur something about "parlor" and noted that he was giving a series of instructions to the clerk. She could not repress a smile. Warren certainly knew how to take charge.

He came back to fetch Meredith with a key in his hands, having managed to turn over the rest of their "baggage" to a bellhop. They whooshed in the elevator to the Imperial floor at the top of the hotel, and the bellhop ushered them into a large suite decorated in ivory and soft gold. After showing them the controls for the television and stereo, the bellhop said, "I'll be back shortly to get your clothes for the valet. Can I do anything else for you, sir?"

Warren handed over what looked like an enormous tip. "I left instructions at the desk," he answered.

Meredith huddled near the door, not wanting to track across the plush white carpeting with her wet feet. The sitting room of the suite was furnished with a low-slung velvet sofa and love seat, both the soft, delicate gold of a sun-drenched beach. Meredith quickly averted her eyes from the doorway opening into a bedroom beyond.

"You can take off your clothes in the bathroom," Warren said in a matter-of-fact voice. "Housekeeping is sending up some sheets for you to wrap yourself in. Just throw your wet things through the door and I'll give them to the porter when he comes back up."

Meredith simply stood there. Acutely aware of being alone in a hotel room with Warren, the awkwardness of the situation hit her full blast. How was he able to remain so poised, the master of any situation? She felt like a naïve schoolgirl.

He gave her a gentle prod, as if he could read her mind. "Go ahead. I'll take care of your things for you."

"What about your—"

"I'll use the other bathroom." He walked across the room and went through the door into the bedroom.

Meredith stepped into the bathroom and peeled off her wet clothing down to bare skin. Then she carefully folded each piece and made a neat stack of her skirt, blouse, slip, bra, and panties. She cracked the door open just a bit and peeked out to be sure that Warren was still in the bedroom. She opened the door and placed the stack of clothing on the floor, retreating quickly into the bathroom. She picked up her stockings, damp and snagged from the barefoot run, and swished them out in the sink. Deciding that with the humidity they would never drip dry, she rolled them in one of the towels and squeezed out as much water as she could before hanging them over the shower rod. All of these chores she did mechanically, like an automaton. She did not dare let herself think about the situation.

There was a soft tap at the door. "Meredith, here are some sheets for you." She opened the door just enough for Warren to hand her the sheets, and when she reached out to take them, their fingers touched.

"Thank you," she said, quickly pushing the door shut. Her heart was pounding. She put the sheets on the lavatory vanity and looked at herself in the mirror. Her formerly chic hairdo was bedraggled and watersoaked, and the rain had pretty much destroyed her makeup. Meredith pulled the pins out of her hair and shook it loose, then got in the shower and turned on the warm water full blast.

Along with its tiny cakes of soap, the hotel provided a small sample bottle of shampoo, and Meredith worked up a foamy lather and scrubbed vigorously, then wrapped a towel turban-style around her head. She stayed in the shower, soaping her smooth skin and letting the warm water spray against her until she felt some of her tension go away. When she felt fresh and clean, she climbed out of the shower and toweled herself dry. She unfolded the crisp white sheet Warren had handed her and draped it over one shoulder, then tucked it at the waist to form a reasonably modest sarong.

She wished she had a blow-dryer. Her long hair would take forever to dry. She removed the wet turban and began to blot it with another towel. She would have to let her hair hang loose until it air-dried. She took a deep breath. She was going to have to go back out there. She had stalled as long as she could. She unlocked the door and stepped out.

Warren was sitting at one end of the long sofa watching the television news. He had opened the drapes and she could see rain beating against the windows and lightning flashing across the sky.

Warren looked up when Meredith walked across the room. "I wondered if you were going to stay in there all night," he said with a smile. "You look like a Greek goddess in that toga."

Thank goodness for his noncommittal tone. He was wrapped with a towel around his waist, his darkly tanned chest completely bare. Dark, curly hair matted his chest and legs. Meredith felt a blush rising in her cheeks and glanced away. "I suspect I look like Neptune rising from the sea with my hair all wet," she said, trying to laugh. "I have a brush in my purse. Do you know where it is?"

"I think I put it on the dresser in the bedroom," Warren said, starting to rise.

"Don't get up," Meredith said hastily. "I'll find it." She did not notice Warren's amused grin. She went into the bedroom and snapped on the light, to find that the same gold and white color scheme was repeated there. Her eyes were drawn to the heavy brocade of the spread on the king-sized bed. She padded barefoot on the soft carpeting and retrieved her brush, her eyes still fixed on the bed. Crazy, jumbled thoughts filled her brain.

"Do you want to hear the latest weather report?" Warren called from the sitting room. Meredith was glad to have her thoughts interrupted. She hurried back into the other room and sat down on the love seat across from Warren to watch the weather bulletin.

The storm system was wreaking havoc all across central Texas, with flash floods in almost every county between San Antonio and Austin. The front was still expected to move through the area by 3:00 A.M., but until then, residents were urged to remain indoors.

"I wonder how long it will take for the water to go down?" Meredith asked.

"Not long after the rain stops. A few hours, maybe."

"When do you think we'll be able to leave?"

"Not until morning."

"Oh." Meredith felt a strange, gnawing sensation in her stomach.

"Does that bother you?" Warren asked, his voice very soft.

"Oh, no." She swallowed hard. "Better to be in here where we're warm and dry."

"With room to stretch our legs," Warren added with a grin. "We're here for the duration, so we might as well make the best of the situation." Meredith strained her ears to discern whether there was any kind of suggestion in his tone, but his voice seemed completely casual. "Maybe there will be something decent on the late show."

Meredith crossed her slim legs and leaned back into a more comfortable position, rearranging the sheet to keep herself covered. If Warren was going to sit there acting like it was perfectly ordinary for the two of them to be sitting, scantily dressed, in a hotel room in the middle of the night, why should she sit stiffly erect on the edge of the sofa? It had been a long, full day, and she was tired. She snuggled into the velvety softness of the sofa, still brushing her hair. Across from her Warren struck a match and lit a cigarette. He leaned his head back against the pillows and inhaled deeply, then exhaled the smoke toward the ceiling, propping his feet on top of the coffee table. Meredith stole a glance in his direction and quickly looked away. There was so much tanned flesh revealed by his skimpy towel that it was hard to concentrate on the sports news. She shifted uneasily on the love seat and pulled her toga sheet around her, as if by keeping her body tightly wrapped she could exercise control over her mind. At this moment she was oblivious to the world of sports and consumed with the presence of Warren, so ruggedly handsome and so intoxicatingly near.

The theme music for the late show marked the end of the news, and Meredith prayed for a comedy or mystery to defuse the magnetic charge of the hotel room. The credits rolled for a 1959 film starring Montgomery Clift and Lee Remick.

"Have you seen this one before?" Warren asked.

"*Wild River?* Never heard of it."

"Shall we try something else?" He idly ruffled his fingers through his dark, thick hair.

"Let's see what *Wild River* is about."

Warren walked over to a lamp table in the corner of the room where there was a tray brought up by room service while Meredith was in the shower. "How about a glass of white wine?" Warren asked, pouring one for himself. "It's not very cold but they sent us some ice."

"That would be nice," Meredith replied. She was

hypnotized by the towel around Warren's waist, which seemed to be sliding almost imperceptibly downward. He snapped the light to a dimmer setting.

"Too much glare on the TV screen," he said casually, walking toward her with the glass. He handed it to her and their fingers touched. Warren lightly clinked his glass against hers in a toast. "To seminars, riverboats and rainstorms," he said with an engaging grin.

Meredith was flustered and quickly took a sip of her wine. "It's very nice," she said.

"Glad you like it. It's my favorite California wine." He walked back toward the other sofa and flopped down. Meredith hoped he wouldn't get up again. It was disconcerting every time he got up and down because his towel seemed in imminent danger of coming loose.

The movie soon got their attention and they were caught up in the story set in the Depression of a woman trying to keep her grandmother's home from being condemned by the authorities for the Tennessee Valley Authority project. Lee Remick was the beautiful granddaughter and Montgomery Clift was the TVA employee whose job it was to remove the houses which stood in the way of the project. Despite their antagonism, the two fell in love, and their romantic scenes were so torrid that Meredith's heart beat faster just watching them.

"I didn't know they did love scenes like this back then," Warren said. "How do you suppose they got past the censor?"

"I wasn't paying attention," Meredith lied.

Warren smiled to himself in the semi-darkness of the room. Meredith was endearingly transparent at times.

A sudden bolt of lightning pierced the sky, followed immediately by a loud noise and then the television set went dead. "Oh, oh. Must have hit the transformer at the TV station," Warren said. He got up and turned the dial, but all the channels were out. He switched the dial to radio and picked up a soft music station.

"I guess we'll never find out how the movie ended," Meredith said with a mournful catch in her voice.

"I thought you weren't paying attention."

"I was dozing part of the time. But I was interested in the story."

"Want some more wine while I'm up?" he asked, holding out his hand for her glass. She nodded but could not look at him. "You know, the characters in the movie reminded me of us," Warren said thoughtfully, pouring the wine. "Except that you're more beautiful than Lee Remick."

Meredith was taken aback. "Why do you say we're like them?" she asked.

"Because we're always fighting over *issues*. You're on the side of the individual and I'm on the side of the state, and we never can agree. And our fights get in the way . . ." He walked back across the room and handed Meredith her glass. Their fingers met, held.

"In the way of what?" Meredith croaked. Something was caught in her throat.

Warren's dark eyes swept over her. His thumb massaged her wrist. "The attraction." His voice was very, very soft.

Meredith's other hand crept to her breast and tugged the sheet higher, as if to protect her body from his devouring eyes. "I hadn't—"

"Don't lie, Meredith." His fingers, warm and gentle, moved up her wrist and stroked her arm, her shoulder. She lifted the glass to her lips and drank. He towered above her, so close she was aware of nothing else but his presence and the softly stirring music of violins. Meredith tilted back her head and drained her glass.

"Warren," she whispered. A delicious warmth spread through her body and she reached out her arms.

He took her glass and carefully set it on the coffee table, as though it were of tremendous importance that it be balanced precisely. He seemed to be concentrating on the very molecules of the table. A muscle twitched at his jaw.

"Warren."

He turned. There was a white line around his mouth. "Oh, God," he groaned. He knelt beside her and buried his face in her soap-scented hair. Her hands crept up his back, delighting in the lean hardness of his body. Her fingers found the thick hair at the base of his neck and stroked it gently. Warren's arms closed around her, pulling her face against the warmth of his bare chest. Her fingers moved around and toyed with the curly hair which matted his chest, as if she could not get enough of the feel of him. She could hear his heart pounding against her ear and wondered if her own heart was pounding with the same wild rhythm. Meredith's lips formed the mystic smile of a woman who knows she has aroused a man's passion. The past and the future did not exist. For now, this joyful moment of the present, Warren was hers completely. The heat from his passion melted all her lingering doubts. His arms held her tenderly, carefully, as if the moment were too precious to hurry.

"Meredith," he whispered, his fingers entwining themselves in her hair and pulling her head back. Her breath quickened, intoxicated by her desire and by her power over him. She lifted her lips for his kiss.

His mouth came down, gently brushing her lips, as if it were the first, tentative kiss of a shy lover. The languid heat which pulsed through her body grew more urgent, and she realized that Warren was playing with her, that she was as much his slave as he was hers. He would not let her have the upper hand, nor would he surrender his power until she surrendered hers.

"Warren, don't tease," she murmured.

"Am I?" he said, chuckling softly against her ear.

Her fingers stroked the muscles in his chest. Her lips, hungry for the taste of him, nibbled gently at his ear.

"You smell so nice," he said, stroking her silky, blonde hair. "Like soap and perfume . . . and woman."

Her fingers gripped the solid muscles in his forearm and pulled his body closer to hers. The sheet which was draped around her shoulder slipped loose. Warren's hands moved from behind her, exposing the creamy flesh of her breasts. He uttered a low moan and buried his face in her exquisite softness. His hands stroked, caressed, became more urgent, lifted a rosy-tipped mound to his eager mouth.

Shivers of delight shot through Meredith's body. She shifted her weight and offered him her other breast. His lips became more demanding until Meredith's body became a lake of molten fire. She lifted his head, knowing that she was at the breaking point. His mouth, hungry now for the fill of her, at last claimed her mouth in an endless, consuming kiss which held back nothing. He jerked the sheet away from her and pulled her onto the floor beside him.

She lay beside him, exulting in her nakedness, glad for him to take his delight in her. His hands and mouth explored, searched, bringing her body to a tingling excitement that demanded satisfaction. Her soft hair lay in waves around her face, and he could see that her eyes glistened with desire. "Warren," she whispered.

His lips cut off the words in her throat. His head pressed her against the floor and his mouth opened over hers, begging for her tongue to respond. His hands, guided by the sure instincts of a practiced lover, fondled her breasts, moved down to stroke her stomach, then slipped to the soft skin of her inner thighs. His mouth begged hers to fulfill its unspoken promises, and his tongue probed and danced until Meredith could think of nothing except the desire which swept her body in a flood of passion. She reached out blindly and pulled the towel from around his waist. She could no longer bear for anything to separate them.

"Meredith," he whispered, his lips moving to nuzzle her neck with a delicious pressure that drove her wild. "Let me—"

She drew his mouth back to her breasts and moaned with pleasure from his gentle kisses. His mouth grew more demanding, and an ache spread through her loins. She reached for his hand and gripped it fervently as waves of passion built to a frenzy inside her, seeking release. She felt that she was straining to hold back a tide that wanted nothing except to be free. With a lover's secret delight, Warren continued to hold her hand, feeling in her frantic grip the urgent response of her body to his. Her back arched, and at exactly the right moment, Warren slipped on top and entered her, riding her crest to its moment of wild, surging satisfaction. He thrust himself deep within her, ignited now by her flaming desire, and they locked themselves in a desperate rhythm which carried them past the far edge of desire until their senses exploded in spasms that carried them to the heights of ecstasy.

Warren gently lifted Meredith from the floor and carried her into the bedroom. She twined her arms around his neck and gave him a sleepy smile. He pulled back the brocade spread and tucked her into the covers, his movements tender and loving. "Go to sleep," he whispered, brushing her cheek with a light kiss. He turned out the light and started back into the sitting room.

"Warren?"

"Ummm?"

"Aren't you coming to bed?"

"In a little while."

Meredith sat up. "What's wrong?" she asked.

"Nothing. I'm just going to have a cigarette."

She lay back down and snuggled into the covers. "Don't be long," she said.

She dozed briefly, but Warren was not there when she woke up. "Warren?" she called sleepily. She had no idea what time it was or how long she had slept.

"I'm right here," he answered from the other room.

"Please come to bed."

"Okay." She was too sleepy to notice the reluctance in his voice. He came into the bedroom and stood beside her in the darkness, looking down at the soft form of her body with an infinite tenderness.

She reached out her hand to him. "Please come to bed."

He crawled in beside her and held her close against him, their bodies naked against each other. Satisfied now, they felt not the blistering heat of desire but the reassuring warmth of spent passion. Meredith slept peacefully in Warren's arms, oblivious to the fact that he lay awake for hours.

She woke to the sound of the shower running in the bathroom and the smell of fresh coffee. She opened her eyes to the unfamiliar room, and the memory of what had happened washed over her. She climbed out of bed and went to look out the window to find that the storm was over and the sun was shining. She greeted the sun with a dazzling smile. "Shame on you," she whispered.

"You went and hid yourself and look what happened." Meredith wrapped her arms around herself and hugged herself with sheer pleasure. It was wonderful to be young and happy . . . and in love. She was radiant with joy.

The door opened behind her, and she turned to smile at Warren, who was coming into the room already fully dressed. Her smile faded at the dark expression on his face.

"The valet sent our clothes back, and breakfast is here," he said, pretending that nothing had happened between them and that it was a perfectly normal occurrence for them to wake up in the same room.

"Warren, is something wrong?" Meredith asked, her face troubled.

"Why don't you get dressed and then let's talk," he suggested. Meredith looked down at her naked body. Suddenly she was embarrassed and reached ineffectually for something to cover herself with. "I'll wait in the other room," he said. "Your clothes are in the bathroom."

Meredith stumbled past him, an incoherent anxiety flooding her thoughts. She quickly showered and dressed, wondering what on earth had happened. Warren seemed angry and she could not understand why. She brushed her hair, and since she had no makeup with her, had to be satisfied with a natural look. She shrugged into the creamy silk blouse and coffee-colored skirt which she had been so proud to wear yesterday because she knew she looked her prettiest. This morning she did not feel pretty. She blew her nose and hoped she would not start crying.

There was no point in delaying any longer. With a troubled heart Meredith went back into the sitting room. She was too embarrassed to look at the floor where last night she and Warren had made love. She gingerly perched on the edge of the sofa and folded her hands in her lap like a naughty child. Warren had refolded into a neat stack the sheet and towels which had served as their clothing the night before, and she averted her head from the reminder of their passion.

"Would you care for some coffee?" he asked politely.

"Please." She took the cup he handed her with an exaggerated care that their fingers not touch. She did not know whether she would be able to swallow, but she desperately needed the hot liquid. She felt as if she were freezing into a pillar of ice.

She sipped her coffee while Warren paced the room waiting for her to finish. The tension became almost unbearable. They did not look at one another and yet they were acutely aware of each other's presence. It seemed incredible that the room could look exactly the same when everything else had changed. Meredith set down her cup with a loud clatter.

Warren sat down on the sofa across from her and pressed his head into his hands. There was a long, painful silence.

"Warren, will you please tell me what's wrong?" She could stand it no longer. She gripped the arm of the love seat.

He lifted his head and met her eyes for the first time. His face was drawn, and gold flecks no longer danced in the dark fires of his eyes. "I want you to know I regret . . . what happened last night," he paused to brace himself. "And I offer my apologies for my behavior—"

Apologize? Regret what happened? "Warren," Meredith interrupted in alarm. "What are you talking about? Last night wasn't *your* fault, we both . . ."

A pained expression passed over his face. He lifted his hand to stop her words. "It shouldn't have happened," he continued. "I blame myself." His avowed intention to keep their relationship casual had been swept away in last night's raging tide of passion, but he would not let it happen again.

Meredith stood, a frown creasing her brow.

"I ask you to forget that it ever happened," he said.

Forget? How could she? A sharp pain pierced her heart and broke it in two. She bowed her head, but his words continued, relentless.

"To do otherwise would only . . . complicate our professional relationship."

"Warren, you can't mean this," she cried, her voice full of agony.

"I'm very sorry," he said, his voice cold and empty. "I've known for weeks that it wouldn't work. It's a compromising position for both of us. There's no way to mix business with pleasure without hurting both our careers."

"Mix business with pleasure," Meredith said, her voice rising. "Is that what you call what we had last night?" For the moment her hurt feelings were submerged by a wave of outrage. "Can't you be honest with yourself and admit that you're really afraid of getting involved?" The red-hot fury in her voice scorched the air between them.

"Meredith, please," Warren said, trying to evade the truth in her statement. He wanted to close out their relationship in a tidy package rather than this clumsy scene. He rose from the sofa and moved quickly to take Meredith's shoulder.

"Keep your hands off me," she cried.

"You're upset, Meredith. Calm yourself down."

"Calm down? Like you? Be cold and logical and

never feel anything? Is that what you want? Sorry, Warren, I don't want to be a block of ice like you, able to turn my feelings on and off like they were a faucet. You're afraid of getting involved, so you tune people out. You send them away and lock up your feelings. That's what you did with the defendant who killed his wife, you couldn't trust yourself or any other defendant after he let you down. Now you're doing the same thing to me. You got scared because you felt too much last night so now you're sending me away because you don't trust yourself where I'm concerned." Meredith's words came thick and fast, in a stream of fury. Warren paled.

"Meredith, you and that defendant are two separate people and two entirely different situations. You're deliberately trying to confuse the issue."

"It's not two different issues, Warren, can't you understand that? That's the whole point, it's exactly the same thing."

"You're wrong, Meredith. I told you in the beginning that we have to keep our personal and our professional relationship separate, but you absolutely refuse to do it."

"Look at me, Warren," she demanded, her eyes bright with anger. "I'm one woman standing here. You're one man. What kind of mental gymnastics do you have to go through in order to split us into a personal self and a professional self?"

"I'd give anything to deal with Meredith Jennings, the professional probation officer, this morning, instead of this hot-tempered female who can probably be heard three blocks away," he said, his jaw so taut the words could hardly escape his throat.

"And I'd give anything to deal with Warren Baxter, the man who is capable of real passion, instead of a cold fish who can't feel anything."

Warren held his breath and counted silently until he could regain control of himself. When he spoke again his voice was devoid of any emotion. "I'm very sorry," he said. "I didn't intend for any of this to happen. I didn't *want* it to happen. Can we just try to forget—"

He didn't *want* it to happen? Forget something so wonderful? A spasm of regret gripped Meredith. Trembling with hurt pride, she grapped her purse and ran from the hotel room.

Chapter Ten

Sheer anger got Meredith through the next week. She had driven back to Austin alone on Saturday morning, her head whirling. Warren had upset her so much that she couldn't remember half of what he'd said to her. She had gone back to work in a blaze of glory because probation officers from the seminar had been quick to congratulate Harvey Gilstrap on her performance. No one suspected that she and Warren had been detained in San Antonio due to the storm, yet Meredith could think of nothing else except the night they had spent together. Her mind was full of thoughts of Warren—his touch, his kiss. He had awakened her body to passion and it continued to betray her with demands for satisfaction despite his brutal rejection of her. She hated him for making her feel so miserable. And yet . . .

And yet she wanted him still. Her body clamored for his skilled touch even as her soul longed for his tenderness. He had made her feel cherished and precious—for a brief while. What had gone wrong? She went over every minute of their time together, probing her wounded heart for an answer.

Apparently he blamed her for the gossip which was detrimental to their careers. Could it be that he thought she was a liability to him? That she stood in the way of his ambitions for the future? Bitterly she thought she was better off without him if he were that self-centered. But if she was better off without him, why did she have this horrible aching emptiness in her heart? She glanced down at the scratch pad on her desk, where she had unconsciously doodled a man's figure in a swirling black robe. Defiantly she added horns to the head, then wadded it into a tight ball and pitched it into the wastebasket. "Devil!" she muttered to herself.

"Who, me?" roared Harvey Gilstrap, his voice protesting innocence. "What kind of welcome is that for Austin's next 'Boss-of-the-Year'?"

"Why, Harvey, what brings you out to the boondocks?" Meredith smiled a welcome despite her surprise. Harvey's cherubic dimples could brighten anyone's day.

"Meredith, I've got a big surprise for you," he boomed cheerfully. "Are you about ready to come back downtown?"

Downtown? Where she would see Warren frequently? God forbid. "Oh, I don't know, Harvey. I really like it at the branch," she answered noncommittally.

"You've got the Community Service project off the ground, now, so somebody else can carry the ball. I'm getting a new office all fixed up for you downtown."

"New office? What's wrong with my old office?"

"Oh, it's not going to be big enough for your new job."

"New job?" Her heart almost stopped beating.

"Surprise, Meredith! The judges voted this afternoon to make you the new Director of Special Services. Special post, created just for you! How about that?"

"But why?"

"Because of the fine job you've done for Travis County. The judges called it your 'creative approach to problem-solving' and think there's lots more you can do. A woman with ideas like yours can go places, Meredith, and the judges want you to have all the opportunity and responsibility you can handle. I sat right there and heard them say it."

"Why, Harvey, that's wonderful."

"That's just what I told the judges when they told me about it at the meeting today."

"Oh, you mean you didn't know ahead of time?"

"Nobody knew. Those judges, they play their cards close to their chests."

"I wonder where they got the idea?" She couldn't resist a fleeting hope that it was Warren who had suggested the new job. No matter how bleak their personal relationship, she still wanted his professional respect.

"They said one of the county commissioners came up with the idea after she heard about the governor appointing you to the task force and all. She talked to some of the judges until she found one who would listen."

"Who was that?" Meredith held her breath for the answer.

"It was Judge Hillebrand first, and then, after the good job you did in San Antonio last week, why, it was clear sailing."

Meredith winced at the mention of San Antonio. "Well, I really appreciate their confidence in me. I'll try to do a good job and make them proud."

"Oh, sure you will. They know that. That's why the vote was almost unanimous."

"*Almost* unanimous?" A warning bell clanged in Meredith's mind.

"Yep. Gol-dang, gal, you've really got support. Why, they voted for you 7-1. And Judge Baxter'll come around when he sees what a good job you do. You'll prove him wrong about not being mature enough for such a big job."

Not mature enough! Warren had actually said that to the other judges? Or was it really because of his fears for his blue-blooded name if the gossips linked it to hers? A new flood of anger swept through her, carrying so much blood to her head that her fingertips tingled. How could Warren be so selfish and unfair? She had *earned* the new job with all her months of hard work. How could he let his anxiety about his precious reputation make him vote against her for something that she deserved on merit. His personal rejection of her had been bad enough, but this professional rejection was too much. She slumped in her chair, the injustice of it sapping her strength.

"Meredith?" Harvey's shiny face looked perplexed. "The judges want you to start June 1st. That will give you time to clean up any odds and ends."

Meredith reached out and patted Harvey's hand. How could she make him understand? "Harvey, as I said earlier, I appreciate the judges' confidence in me, but I'd rather stay here at the branch. There's still a lot to do here."

"Hell's bells, Meredith, this is your big chance. Have you lost your hearing?"

"No, not my hearing." She smiled in spite of herself at the incredulous look on Harvey's face. "Just my mind."

"That's obvious." Harvey stiffened and tried to assume the persona of a stern supervisor. "Judges are not accustomed to having other people tell them *no*. What reason can you offer for your unwise and hasty decision?"

"Let's just say it's personal." Her eyes dropped to her hands, clenched in her lap.

"You're not getting off that easy, Meredith. Tell old Harvey what's the matter."

Meredith tried to evade Harvey's eyes, but the force of his honest confusion overwhelmed her. "Oh, Harvey, it's too complicated to explain."

"Let me guess," he said. "Everything was fine until I opened my big mouth and blabbed that Judge Baxter didn't vote for you." He watched carefully as the telltale pink rushed to her face. "And there has been a mite of courthouse gossip about the two of you."

Meredith squirmed in her chair but kept her eyes downcast.

"Well?" Harvey leaned back and folded his hands across his plump belly while he made little clicking noises with his tongue.

"That's it, Harvey. It's all the gossip. People blow things all out of proportion. And Warren blames me for it. That's the real reason he didn't vote for me. It had absolutely nothing to do with my professional capabilities. He doesn't care whether I can do the job or not. All he cares about is his precious reputation and whether I might hurt him in the next election." Her voice was slowly rising and Harvey cocked an eye at the open door.

"Ssh," he cautioned. "You don't want everybody to hear you."

"Don't you see, Harvey? That's exactly what I'm talking about. There's no such thing as personal privacy in a job like this. It's just not worth it. It's even worse at the courthouse downtown. Tell the judges thanks, but no thanks. I'm staying here."

Harvey was shocked into a rare silence. Meredith expected *him* to deliver a refusal to the judges? Woefully he remembered the Greek tragedies he had been forced to read in college, with their autocratic kings who put to death any messenger who brought bad news. The similarities between district judges and Greek kings made him cringe, and his instinct for self-preservation generated a sudden burst of adrenalin. "Now, Meredith," he crooned. "You don't want to make a hasty decision that you'll regret later. Why don't you just go home for the rest of the day and get your mind off things for a while?" He urged her to her feet, awkwardly patting her on the back.

He was so transparent that Meredith would have laughed if she hadn't been so angry. Poor Harvey, all he wanted was a world safe for him so he could keep his cherubic smile in place. He could never be comfortable with Meredith on one side of him and eight district judges on the other. A fellow could get killed in the crossfire. "You go home and think things over," he coaxed. "You'll feel different after you've had a good night's sleep. We'll talk about it tomorrow." He scooted out the door and into the next office before Meredith could say another word.

Meredith reached in the battered file cabinet for her purse and picked up a couple of files from the desk. She might as well go home, she thought self-pityingly. How could she work when her mind was in such a confused whirl? Damn you, Warren Baxter, she thought, to ruin what could have been one of the happiest days of my life. The tightness in her throat began to spread, and a warmth behind her eyes made her blink. She stopped at the reception desk to say that she would be gone for the rest of the afternoon but had to wait while Brenda took an interminable telephone call.

In her distress, Meredith did not realize that Brenda was intentionally dawdling at Harvey's direct instruction. Finished at last, in her desire to escape the office Meredith practically bolted down the steps. She was almost running to her car when she heard a horn honking and a car roaring down the street behind her. She turned to see Warren's silver Mercedes screech to a stop beside her, and he jumped out and loped to the sidewalk.

She had not seen him since she stormed out of their hotel room in San Antonio, and bitter confusion swept through her. It was too much. She was just not up to coping with Warren right now.

Nor was he ready to cope with her. But Harvey had given him no choice, and Warren was dragged into the situation despite his intense desire to disentangle himself from the problems of an involvement with Meredith. Yet he admired her competence and valued the contribution she was making to the community. He could not let her antagonism toward him hinder her career—especially since a refusal to accept the promotion would give courthouse tongues something new to gossip about. Warren snorted in disgust to find himself trapped by circumstances.

"What do you think you're doing?" he shouted angrily.

"None of your business," she retorted.

He took her arm and pulled her close to his side. "It was less than two hours ago that the Travis County judges showed their confidence in you by voting you into a brand-new position. What's the big idea of giving up before you even get started?"

"How did you know?"

"Harvey called me the minute he stepped out of your office. Thank goodness for once he showed good judgment."

"Good judgment? He's a big blabbermouth if you ask me."

"Well, I didn't happen to ask you." He opened the car door and gave her a gentle shove. "Get in," he commanded.

Meredith was too upset to argue, and people on the street were beginning to stare. There had been too much gossip already, and it wouldn't do to stir up any more. She got in the car and sat stiffly erect while Warren got in on the driver's side and pulled into the traffic. They drove through the Austin streets arguing for an hour, with Warren reminding Meredith that her work as a probation officer was important and that she had earned a great deal of recognition in a relatively short period of time. Meredith alternately sulked and stormed, afraid to tell Warren the real reason for refusing the new job. To let him find out how much his rejection mattered would make her vulnerable. In order to keep the discussion on a professional basis, she stubbornly insisted that she preferred to work with individual probationers rather than to fill an administrative position. There was enough truth in what she said to sound convincing, but Warren neglected to mention that Harvey had already given him her real reason. When she cooled off, maybe he could change her mind.

It was a beautiful afternoon in early May, and finally both Meredith and Warren abandoned their argument to pay attention to the azaleas and lilacs in full bloom throughout the city. The Mercedes seemed to choose its own route, and after a time they found themselves on Highway 71 headed east. They entered the Hill Country, where the countryside was ablaze with fields of bluebonnets, Indian paintbrush, brown-eyed Susans, buttercups, and other spring wildflowers. The sky, so often hazy in this part of Texas, today was a bright, clear blue with fluffy white clouds. In the face of nature's splendor, their voices grew quieter and then fell altogether. How could they continue to argue in such a beautiful world? Outside Bastrop they began to smell the unmistakable fresh scent of pine trees, and Warren rolled down his window so the car could fill with the pungent fragrance. He turned off the highway onto a farm-to-market road that cut through a grove of ancient pines, and after a long, bumpy ride they stopped at a gate in a neat rail fence.

Warren got out of the car and unlocked the gate, then motioned to Meredith to drive the car through the opening. He closed and locked the gate behind her, then got back in the car and drove it across narrow ruts to a barn-like structure made of dark, weathered wood.

"Where are we?" Meredith asked. She had thought they were driving aimlessly.

"This is my family homeplace," Warren answered. "We were so near, I thought I might as well show it to you." Live oak trees at least a century old surrounded the building, and when they got closer, Meredith could see that an old barn had been converted to a home. A tractor tire was suspended from an oak branch to make a swing big enough for two people, and in the meadow beyond there was a pond fed by an underground stream. Black-and-white cows grazed on the lush native grass, and the silence was broken only by moos of contented pleasure. Peering closer into the setting sun, Meredith could see a gangly-legged brown colt nursing at its mother's side.

Warren led her up the steps onto a wooden deck that circled the house. Bluebonnets were as thick as a carpet all the way to the pond. Warren slid back the wooden shutters that protected the windows and unlocked the kitchen door. "Come in and look around," he said.

The barn-like exterior did not prepare Meredith for the comfortable interior of the house. It was patterned after a New England barn, with a loft upstairs, and downstairs there was a huge, open living-and-dining area with plank floors and open-beam walls. A huge native-stone fireplace formed the center wall of the house, and off to either side were a large, roomy kitchen with every modern convenience and a large bedroom suite complete with television set and Jacuzzi. Patchwork quilts hung from the balcony rail upstairs, and shelves on the walls contained a fine collection of antique duck decoys. Meredith climbed up the stairs to the loft and found two additional bedrooms there, each decorated with heirloom counterpane spreads on the brass beds. In an open study area an oak chest held a collection of pewter hollowware that looked like it might be priceless. She skipped back down the stairs, her face lit with pleasure.

"It's beautiful, Warren. How can you bear to leave it and go to Austin?"

"Because I have to. My work is in Austin," he answered. "I come back as often as I can."

"Who takes care of it for you?"

"I have a foreman. He lives down the road and watches over it as if it were his own." Warren paused, then added, "Sometimes it seems like it's more his than mine because I'm here so seldom."

They walked back out on the deck and sat down on a wooden porch swing to watch the sunset, streaks of crimson and pink against the darkening sky.

Meredith was struck by the change that came over Warren with the change in his environment. Here in the place where he grew up he was completely at ease. She had never seen him like this before, or felt so close to him. She felt that she could ask him anything. "Warren, why did you leave here?"

He thought for a while before he answered her. In the silence they could hear mockingbirds singing and crickets chirping. Occasionally an airplane passed overhead too far away to hear.

"I guess it was because I'm so restless," he said at last. "I love it here, but the pace is too slow for me. I'm a mover and a shaker, Meredith. I have to be where the action is. But you know," he added thoughtfully, "I don't think I ever get very far away. My roots are here, and this place is in my blood. It's the way I think life ought to be for everybody."

Meredith thought of life in Houston where she had grown up, a sprawling urban cancer devouring the land. She wondered if Warren could understand people who had never owned a roof over their heads, let alone a picturesque farm. It changed people when they lived a crowded existence, packed into small areas where they were perpetually bombarded with noise and sensation and where they were only renters of space they could never own. How could people put down roots in such a hostile environment? "I thought I was the naïve one, Warren," she replied, "but you're more innocent than I am. You must be the last remnant of early America."

"Naïve? Me?" The shocked disbelief on Warren's face was visible even in the fading daylight.

"When people live like this, they can be independent and self-reliant. Rugged individualism thrives." Meredith's voice was soft and thoughtful. "But in the cities, people can't control their lives the way you do here. They become victims instead of achievers."

"They don't have to," he argued. "*You* didn't, and you grew up in a city. Look what you've accomplished."

The pride in his voice brought a lump to Meredith's throat. "I'm one of the lucky ones," she whispered.

"No, Meredith, you're one of the *plucky* ones," he insisted. "You're just like me. You believed that you could make something out of your life, and you did it."

Meredith turned her head away so that he could not see the tears that trickled down her cheeks. He didn't understand her at all, and she didn't know whether she dared to try to make him understand. Her long-buried secret might drive him away forever. What did he know of life at the bottom of the social ladder?

"All it takes is hard work," Warren continued. "If everybody threw themselves into their work the way you do, they would be getting promotions and raises."

She raised her hands to her face and wiped away the tears that would not stop falling. She would have to tell him. But she had never told anyone before, not ever. She didn't know where to start. Her breath escaped in a quivering sigh.

"Hey, what's wrong?" Warren asked. "You're crying." He reached out his arms for her, but she shook her head and moved to the far corner of the porch swing.

"Give me some room so I can tell you," she whispered.

The tone of her voice stopped Warren. He dropped his arms and leaned back in the swing. "Okay," he said.

It took her a long time to tell all of it, and there were long pauses when she could not talk at all. She sat with her hands clenched in her lap, head bent and eyes staring vacantly at the wooden slats of the deck. She did her best to make him understand about her childhood in the city where there was never enough money because her mother's salary was so small.

"She did her best," Meredith said softly. "There were three of us kids, and our dad deserted us when we were small. Mom worked two jobs when we were little, and when we got bigger, we got jobs, too."

"What kind of jobs?"

"Oh, cleaning houses and sweeping out stores. Selling doughnuts door-to-door, stuff like that."

"How old were you?"

"About ten, I guess. I'm not making excuses, though," she insisted earnestly. "I just want you to know how it was. It was the same way for everybody else, too." After a long pause she continued, "It was when we got to high school that it was the worst, because other kids from the good part of town went there, too, and they had stuff we didn't have. It made us feel shabby. It wasn't so hard to be poor in grade school because everybody else was poor, too, but in high school people could tell who was rich and who wasn't, and then it was awful. I hated to go to school because I couldn't have the kind of clothes that other girls had. It just built up in me until I couldn't stand it any more."

She paused. The hard part was coming.

"So one Saturday I went to the shopping center with some other kids. They had done it before and knew how. They showed me how, too. We got in the dressing room and stole some expensive clothes by putting them on under our own clothes. But I guess I must have looked guilty, because I got caught."

"What happened?" There was nothing but concern in Warren's voice.

"It was awful. They took me to the manager's office and called the police. They asked me a whole bunch of questions and then they took me to the police station and called my mom. She cried and cried and said she didn't know what to do. Some judge appointed a lawyer because we didn't have any money, and he said the best thing was to plead guilty and try for a probated sentence or a detention home. It was so scary, the big courtroom and all those people and my mom crying. She had to miss work to go to court with me and then we didn't have any money for groceries for that week."

The sun had gone peacefully to sleep, completely unaware of Meredith's anguish. The sky was dark now, waiting for the moon.

"The judge put me on probation and assigned me to Mrs. Dickinson. She was wonderful to me. I was ready to quit school and get a full-time job to help my mom, but Mrs. Dickinson wouldn't let me. She made me go to school, and she gave me all kinds of encouragement. She found out about grants, and she called lots of people so I could go to the University of Houston when I graduated from high school. She came out to our house, and she even helped my mom get a better job.

She changed things for us. My life was never the same again after I met Mrs. Dickinson."

"So that's why you're such a tiger of a probation officer," Warren said, whistling softly through his teeth.

"I have to be," she replied. "I owe it to Mrs. Dickinson to do for other people what she did for me. I want to give every single probationer the same chance I got."

Warren opened his arms, and this time Meredith let him pull her close. The sexual intimacy they had experienced in San Antonio was only a pale shadow compared to the satisfying warmth of this emotional intimacy. There were still many unresolved problems in their relationship, but for the moment those could wait. This was not the time to spoil the precious closeness. Meredith leaned her head against Warren's shoulder, his chin resting on her head, and felt perfectly at peace for the first time in her adult life. She had carried her secret for such a long time, and it had grown so very heavy.

Only the whirring of cicadas broke the gentle silence. For now there was nothing else that needed to be said.

"I imagine you're starved," Warren said, after a time.

"Sort of."

"I'll see if I can find us something to eat. Will you settle for canned chili?"

"Anything is fine. I'm too hungry to be choosy."

He stood and pulled Meredith to her feet. In the darkness it was impossible to see his expression, so she had to rely on the tone of his voice. He dropped a casual kiss on her forehead.

"Warren, will you tell me the truth about something?"

"Sure." The boards creaked as he stepped across the deck.

"Why didn't you vote for me on my promotion?"

He flinched. "Because of all the gossip about us." Meredith's head shot up with a sharp retort ready on her lips, but he lifted his hand to quiet her. "But not the way you think. It's just that with all the talk, if I did anything to advance your career, it would be the kiss of death for you. People would say it was because of our, ah, personal relationship—that you traded sexual favors to get yourself promoted."

Meredith was indignant. "But that's not fair. I *earned* that promotion."

"Of course you did. But just to be sure it would be public knowledge that I had nothing to do with it, I fought very hard to keep you from getting the very promotion I wanted you to have. I made quite a point of your youth and inexperience, as a matter of fact." He grinned, quite pleased with the success of his strategy. "And it worked, too. So naturally you'll accept the promotion—just to prove me wrong, of course."

She nodded. "Of course." At last the knot in her stomach unkinked and she drew a shaky breath. "But in the future, Judge, I think it would be only fair if you'd just explain—"

Inside the telephone rang. "What the—" Warren muttered, hurrying into the kitchen, flipping on the light switch as he did so. "Hello," he barked into the receiver. "Harvey? How did you find me? . . . You what? . . . Oh . . . she wants *what?* Okay, I'll tell Meredith." In consternation Warren hung up the telephone and turned to Meredith. "It's one of your probationers, Mary Roberta Stanley. She's gone into labor and asked the hospital to notify you."

"Oh," Meredith murmured, lost in thought. "Then I'll need to go to the hospital right away. She doesn't have any family, and her boyfriend deserted her. I took the Lamaze classes with her and told her I'd be with her when the time came."

Warren's expression was both stupefaction and admiration. "Is there no limit to what you'll do for one of your probationers?"

"Of course there is," she responded sweetly. "Even *I* draw the line somewhere. I absolutely refuse to go to bed with a judge on their behalf."

A soft growl escaped Warren's throat.

"Come on, Judge, I need to go to the hospital. I'm about to become a father."

Chapter Eleven

Warren dropped Meredith at the hospital and went home to his condominium to toss restlessly for several hours while sleep evaded him. Usually when he was with Meredith he was drawn to her by a powerful sexual magnetism that required all his discipline to keep in check. When he lacked the necessary restraint and gave in to the attraction, the results were disastrous. He *knew* he was right, the relationship simply could not work. The gossip that linked their names was too destructive.

Over the years there had been chronic speculation whenever he appeared publicly with a new woman, but he had been able to chalk it up to being a prominent bachelor. It had been frivolous talk that had, if anything, enhanced his reputation. But the talk about himself and Meredith was different because their work converged. Meredith was only dimly aware how exaggerated the rumors had been because Harvey had shielded her from the worst of it. Warren had not been so lucky. He had learned of whispered suggestions that Meredith used her attractions to get preferential treatment for her probationers and that he had compromised his judicial powers in exchange for sexual favors. The odious gossip had damaged their credibility, and the only way to put an end to it was to put an end to their relationship. It would only hurt both of them to continue. And yet there was something about Meredith that tugged at his heart. Tonight, for instance. She was so open, so vulnerable, so painfully honest. . . . It scared him that she could be so willing to give of herself, to give so generously, to him or to her probationers. How could she *care* so much?

His own emotions had been carefully blocked off by a lifetime of logically analyzing choices, weighing the advantages and disadvantages of every situation. Someone like Meredith, who gave first and thought later, posed insoluble problems for a man who had to keep everything under careful control. He ought to put her out of his life and do it now. He *ought* to, before he found himself scorched by her blazing passion for life. But then he remembered her brown eyes full of compassion, her lips curved in a teasing smile. . . . He stubbed out his cigarette and leaned back with a sigh. At length he fell into a fitful sleep, haunted by misty dreams of himself running along the seashore, desperately trying to catch up with a woman who ran ahead of him on the beach. He wanted to cry out to her, but his mouth was bound with a silk handkerchief. Just as he was about to overtake her, she clambered into a boat and set sail, waving goodbye while her laughter floated across the Gulf.

When the shrill ringing of the telephone woke him up, his heart was hammering, his mouth dry and thick. The sound of Meredith's familiar voice was such a welcome relief that he laughed, banishing the dream from his consciousness.

"Warren, guess what! It's a boy, a beautiful baby boy, and Mary Roberta is fine and everything is wonderful. Will you come get me, please?"

It was 5:00 A.M. when Warren went back to the hospital to find Meredith bubbling with excitement over her participation in the birth experience.

"Oh, Warren, she was so brave!" Meredith exulted. "She did just what the doctor said, breathing exactly right. And the baby is such a darling little boy with dark, curly hair. She's going to name him Mark."

Warren grinned to himself. He had never yet known a female who didn't go completely bonkers on the subject of newborn babies. As far as he was concerned, all babies looked alike and he could never understand the gasps of delight over such squirming, squalling, beet-red little creatures.

Meredith caught his sly grin and chastised him. "Just you wait, Warren Baxter," she said. "Your turn will come someday, and you'll be just as excited!"

The very thought gave Warren cold chills. Not him. The thought of spending a night in a labor room made him feel panicky. It was definitely time to change the subject. In the pale light of early dawn he could see that Meredith's clothes were rumpled. "I bet you never did get anything to eat," he said.

"Eat?" She looked at him in surprise. "I forgot all about it. What time is it?"

"A little after five." He tried to think of an out-of-the-way place where nobody would recognize them. "Shall I take you to one of the pancake houses out on I-35 for some breakfast?"

"I'm too sleepy, Warren. Would you mind just taking me home?"

"Do you have anything there to eat?"

"I think so. At least some eggs."

He turned the car toward her street. "I'll cook your breakfast for you. How's that for a royal reward?"

"I don't know," she said dryly. "How well can you cook?"

Warren laughed. "I guess we're going to find out. Maybe we'll be treated to beginner's luck."

The Mercedes slipped into the driveway and Warren insisted that Meredith take a shower and relax while he prepared breakfast for her. He seemed to be relatively harmless in the kitchen, and Meredith was fast nearing the point of exhaustion. She went into the bathroom and drew the water for a bath. A shower would only stimulate her, and she wanted the sheer relaxation of a tub full of bubbles. She poured out a double portion of bath oil and climbed in. Twisting her blonde hair into a knot, she leaned back, sighing with pleasure. She was almost asleep when Warren called that breakfast was ready. Somehow it was just too much trouble to get out of the tub, or even to answer. She lay in the tub in a state of complete lethargy.

He knocked at the bathroom door. "Did you hear me? Breakfast is ready."

"In a little while," she answered, her voice almost too low to hear.

"Breakfast will get cold," he answered with all the indignation of a French chef.

"I'm too tired," she said.

"Meredith, get out of that tub or I'm coming in to get you."

A lazy smile flickered across her lips. She wondered if he really would. Anyway, it was much too nice in her tub of bubbles to get out just yet. She tried to remember whether she had locked the door. Probably not. "Give me a few more minutes," she said, teasing just a little.

"Now."

"No."

The doorknob turned surprisingly easily. She looked adorable with her blonde hair piled on top of her head, her big, brown eyes full of dreamy promises. The bathroom was filled with the fragrance from the bubbles. Warren stepped over the clothes that were strewn across the floor.

"I haven't washed yet," Meredith said. "I'm too tired."

He knelt beside the tub, rolled up his sleeves, and reached for the soft pink washcloth. "I'll wash you," he said. His voice was in perfect control, but there were fires stirring in his eyes. He took the soap from the tray and lathered the washcloth, then gently stroked Meredith's face.

"Don't get soap in my eyes," she said, squeezing them shut.

"I'm going to scrub your ears if you don't behave yourself," he answered. His hands, big and sure of themselves, moved down her neck with the washcloth, then across her shoulders and down her arms. Her skin tingled, and she lay back, her eyes still closed, enjoying the pampering. The washcloth moved under the water beneath the bubbles and stroked her breasts, her stomach, her hips and thighs. She could feel Warren's warm breath against her face and knew that if she opened her eyes he would be within inches of her. She opened her eyes. Their eyelashes brushed, and she lifted her wet arms around his neck and pulled his face down to hers.

"No, you don't, you little vixen," he whispered, moving his mouth away from hers. "I fixed your breakfast and you're going to come eat it before it gets cold."

"It's only food," she said, her lips seeking again.

"But *I* cooked it," he said. "The first time in my life I ever cooked breakfast for a woman." He moved the washcloth down her legs and feet.

"And what about giving a woman a bath?" she asked, a gleam of interest in her eye. "Is this your first time for that, too?"

"Well, no," he said modestly. "Turn around and I'll do your back." She turned, splashing noisily. "Damn it, Meredith, you soaked my shirt."

"Too bad," she said sweetly. "I'm ready to get out now."

He stood to get a towel as she rose from the bubbles, her skin glowing like ivory porcelain. "Oh, God," he whispered, "you're so beautiful." He wrapped the towel around her shoulders and drew her next to him, his hands warm against her face. His lips moved toward hers, but she turned her head.

"I want my breakfast," she said, laughing.

"You tease." He scrubbed her vigorously with the towel and threw it on the floor. "Where's your robe?"

"It should be hanging on the back of the door."

He came back with a gauzy pink gown. "This will have to do." He slipped it over her head and drew it down, brushing his fingers against her breasts as he adjusted the fitted bodice. Meredith was pretty sure her old terry-cloth robe was hanging on the hook, too, and smiled that he had chosen to ignore it.

"Am I properly dressed for breakfast?" she inquired politely.

"Quite," he answered, taking in the soft swell of her breasts above the low-cut bodice and the way the gauze draped along her shapely legs. He lifted her from the tub and carried her to the kitchen. "Eat," he said, setting her down at the table. He got their plates out of the oven where he had been keeping the food warm, and Meredith laughed out loud. The eggs were almost raw and the toast was burned. The fresh grapefruit had unfortunately been included on the plate and was now wilted from the oven's heat. The coffee, at least, was wonderful. She ate every bite, though her giggling seemed to annoy him.

He took off his wet shirt and sat at the table, his head leaning on one arm, watching her eat. She was a mystery to him, a seductress one minute and a laughing child the next. Apparently her present mood was going to last for a while. He picked up his fork and began to wolf down the only breakfast he had ever cooked for a woman. It really wasn't that bad.

"Oh, Warren, it was divine," Meredith said, wiping her mouth with a napkin which hid her grin. "Does my 'royal reward' include washing the dishes?"

"Definitely not. By tomorrow you'll be rested. They can wait until then."

"You're sulking. Did I hurt your feelings?" She could not repress another giggle. She got up and walked barefooted to stand behind his chair and stroke his firm-muscled arms. He tipped up his head and they gazed into each other's eyes upside down. "You're making me dizzy," she whispered.

Warren rose from his chair and stood next to her, his chest bare against her slender arm. Her fingernails gently stroked his back. "That tickles."

"Does it?" she asked innocently, tickling some more. As if that were the cue Warren had been waiting for, he swept her into his arms and buried his face in her neck.

"Oh, Meredith," he murmured.

His arms felt wonderful around her, strong and safe. She snuggled closer against him, her bare shoulders brushing against his chest, and lifted her lips for his kiss.

Warren made love to her with exquisite tenderness, his hands and lips as gentle as if she were made of some ethereal substance too fragile and delicate to touch. Infinitely slow, intoxicatingly sensuous, he stroked and caressed her warm fragrant flesh, silky and eager under his touch. When desire made her face glow with an inner translucence, he lifed her in his arms and carried her into the bedroom, lowering her onto fresh, clean sheets that still retained a fragrance of sun and soap.

Meredith gave herself to him with a joyful surrender, almost as if she sensed that this might be their last time together, her surrender more precious because it was heightened with a sense of finality. She clung to him as though she would never let him go, murmuring his name over and over again. When he fell asleep, she held him in her arms, his head against her breast, and stroked his hair while salty tears trickled down her cheeks.

Warren stirred in her arms. "Come here," he whispered, nuzzling her breast.

Oh, Warren, I love you so! her heart cried, but her

lips were mute. She slipped into his waiting arms and gave the love she could not voice.

It was late afternoon when the telephone rang and woke them up. "Hello," Meredith said sleepily, a question in her voice. "Oh! . . . Yes, Harvey . . . but why?" She sat up and pulled the sheet around her bare shoulders, squinting in the sunlight that streamed through the bedrom window. Warren, awakened too, reached out to trace the shape of her breast under the sheet, giving her an impish smile. "Why, thank you so much," she continued, shaking her head to indicate to Warren that her gratitude was not intended for him. "What time?" she asked, looking at the clock-radio beside the bed. "Yes, that would be very nice. I'll meet you there."

"Come here, you gorgeous blonde," Warren said, reaching for her. She evaded his reach and climbed out of the bed.

"I have to go back to the hospital. The newspaper is coming out to do a story."

Warren's tone was nothing but impudent. "Tell Harvey to go fly a kite. I'm not letting you out of my sight." He climbed out of the bed after her and backed her against the wall, his lips searching for hers. Desire rose in him, blocking out everything else except her intoxicating presence. For the moment the real world did not exist.

"Warren, behave yourself," she protested.

"What do you think I'm doing?" he whispered suggestively, his hands exploring her body. His lips sank into the hollow of her throat, sending tingling sensations up and down her spine. Meredith closed her eyes and forced herself to think about something else.

She had to get control of herself or she would never be able to get dressed for the interview.

"Really, Warren, I certainly can't go get my picture made with a hickey on my neck," she said, her voice as cross and irritable as she could make it.

"You can wear a scarf," he insisted, his mouth continuing its probing.

"Really, Warren, please. I have to get dressed. And so do you. You'll have to take me to the hospital because my car is still at the office."

Warren's hands dropped slowly to his sides. "You want me to take you to the hospital where Harvey's got some news people to do a story on you?"

Meredith shot him a sharp look. There was something odd in his voice. "Do you mind?"

"I think it would be better if I took you to get your car and you went by yourself. It's bad enough that your car was parked at the office all night when everybody knew you left with me."

"Warren, for heaven's sake, Harvey knew I was at the hospital with Mary Roberta all night."

"Not until—what time is it?—three o'clock in the afternoon."

"Oh, Warren, you're acting paranoid. It's Saturday. There's nobody at the office to know my car is still there."

There was a momentary look of relief on his face, but his doubts had spoiled the warmth of the morning. Meredith was only too aware of her nakedness as she stepped around Warren and made her way to the bathroom. She suspected that she made a ridiculous figure stomping from her room without a stitch on. Confusion clawed at her mind with disturbing thoughts, shattering the joy of the previous hours.

The clothing strewn across the bathroom was a tacit reminder of their prior lovemaking. With a lump in her throat, Meredith scooped up the clothes and shoved them into the hamper. She took a quick shower and brushed her teeth before she realized that she would have to go back into the bedroom to get something to wear. She checked the hook on the bathroom door, and sure enough, there was her old terry-cloth robe. She couldn't repress a small, sad smile. She put on the robe and went back into the bedroom, relieved to find that Warren had gone into the kitchen. She could smell fresh coffee perking. "I'm through if you want to get in the bathroom," she called. Hunting in the closet, she found a honey-colored silk shirtwaist dress with a soft leather sash. Harvey had said he would take her to the County Line for dinner after the interview. She shrugged on the dress and decided it was appropriate, being both businesslike and feminine. She leaned toward the mirror to see whether the red mark on her neck showed. It did. She reached for a printed scarf.

Warren emerged from the bathroom, now showered, shaved, and fully dressed. "Your razor leaves a lot to be desired," he complained, searching for the right note. Neither of them seemed to be sure what "etiquette" required in the present circumstances, and Warren's guilt feelings were making him a little edgy. He knew he was wrong to take such private pleasure in Meredith's company when he dreaded the thought of a public appearance. "You look very pretty," he said, trying to rise to the occasion. "Nice scarf."

She attemped a grin. "I hope it photographs well."

The mention of photographers tipped the scales in Warren's mind. Angry with himself for being caught up in an affair with Meredith which was against his best judgment, he directed his irritation toward her.

"You're quite the young lady on her way up, aren't you, Meredith? Only yesterday you were promoted, and already you have a press conference and get your picture in the papers. What about TV? Is Bettis Langley going to be there, too?"

"I really don't know." Meredith felt a gnawing tightness in her stomach. What had gotten into Warren? "Are you trying to pick a fight with me?"

"Not at all. I'm just trying to bring to your attention the fact that you'll be in the public eye as much as I am from now on. It won't be just courthouse gossip any more—it'll be television cameras and the ten o'clock news."

"So what?" Defiance hardened her backbone and made her stubborn. "Are you going to run through your San Antonio lecture again about public image and possible damage thereto? Really, Warren, you certainly have a unique way with women—first you make love to them and then chew them out for not giving you the right professional respect! This is certainly a new experience." Every word dripped sarcasm.

"Knock it off, Meredith. You're imagining slights where none is intended. I realize that discretion is not your stock-in-trade, but you could exercise a little caution. We don't have to broadcast our relationship to the whole wide world."

"I doubt the whole wide world is interested. In fact, I doubt if even one percent of the people in Austin are interested. And furthermore, as far as I'm concerned, we don't have any *relationship* to broadcast!"

"Oh, fine," he answered, throwing up his hands. "Go into hysterics—"

"Now just a minute," Meredith said, her voice dangerously low. "I haven't even raised my voice. I don't know what your problem is, Warren, but there's something seriously wrong with a man who can be warm and tender when he's away from business in San Antonio or out in the Hill Country but turn into an uptight, image-conscious *snob* when he's in the city."

"My only response to that is that it would be delightful if *you* could switch into two identities. Your single role of emotionalism-run-riot is growing very tiresome."

His words stung her enough to bring her to her senses. "Warren, what's happening to us? An hour ago we were in each other's arms. Now here we are at each other's throats!"

Warren wearily rubbed his forehead. The truth in her words made him ashamed of himself. Maybe he was too rigid and overconcerned with appearances. "I'm sorry, Meredith. Come on, I'll take you to the hospital."

"No, really. Just drop me at the office and I'll get my car."

A stern mask settled over his face. His words were clipped. "I said I'd take you to the hospital. Let's go."

If Warren had written a script containing all his worst fears, it would have duplicated the real-life scenario at the hospital. Bettis Langley was already there with a camera crew, so naturally she had to make Warren the focus of her story. The newsman from the rival television station kept the camera on Meredith, but his questions centered on speculation concerning her rapid career rise rather than on her work with probationers. The poor rookie from the newspaper could hardly get in a word edgewise and kept tripping over the camera equipment. Forgotten in the race for a juicy story was Mary Roberta Stanley, the proud new mother who was supposed to be the leading character in the drama.

It took a 253-pound guardian angel to salvage the situation, and when Harvey bellowed, angel-like, the cameras suddenly found their way to Mary Roberta. After Harvey indulged in five minutes of friendly blackmail, the cameras re-shot the story from the proper perspective and the news people promised to "deep-six" the first filming. They packed up their gear and left with one of the tamest stories in weeks, but they ran it anyway since it was the weekend and news was slow.

Even Harvey at his most endearing could not salvage the situation between Meredith and Warren, however. Harvey could only watch helplessly as Meredith said softly, "Go ahead and say 'I told you so.' You're entitled to it."

Warren shrugged. "No need. I've been in politics a long time, and I've learned what to expect. You're new at the game."

"I'm really sorry. If Harvey hadn't come just when he did, our names would be—"

Warren turned to Harvey. "Thanks a lot, Harvey. I owe you one." He turned to go.

"Warren?"

He paused, mid-step. In his ears he could hear the roaring of the sea and a woman's laughter across the water as she sailed away. "Are you coming?" he asked.

"No. Harvey can take me to get my car, and then we're going out to the County Line for a barbecue."

"Would you like to join us?" Harvey asked. "My wife is coming, too."

Meredith interrupted. "No, Warren has other plans." She walked to him and took his hand. It was hard to know which of them had the colder fingers. "I understand now. You're right, it won't work. I should have listened to you in the first place." At last their eyes met, for the first time in interminable minutes, and each was surprised to see the pain etched in the other's. For a moment Meredith gripped Warren's fingers. "Whenever I see a field of bluebonnets, I'll think of you," she whispered. A tear spilled over and slowly trickled down her cheek. He took the silk handkerchief from his breast pocket and wiped it away.

"Goodbye, Meredith," he said softly. There was a strange burning in his eyes.

"Let's not be maudlin," Meredith said, quickly standing on tiptoe and kissing his cheek. "Let's just say 'See you at the top!' " Her laughter echoed in the air as she ran lightly from the hospital lobby, but no one could see her tears. Warren said nothing but lifted his hand as if to call her back, too late. He looked down at the silk handkerchief he was holding and felt nothing but emptiness. Harvey slipped out the side door and left Warren standing there alone.

Chapter Twelve

The beauty of the unfolding spring served only to accentuate Meredith's misery. The riotous colors of the azaleas—pinks, fuchsias, and purples—which in other springs had taken away her breath, now seemed to her like cemetery flowers at a fresh grave. She had done the right thing. She *knew* she had done the right thing. But why did it have to hurt so much.

Her work was terribly important: the rescuing and salvaging of wrecked lives. It was work which needed desperately to be done, and there were few who had the patience, and the sheer grit, to do it. And keep doing it. That was part of the trouble. So many probation officers became discouraged because of the never-ending problems and the infrequent successes which chipped away at their idealism. The turnover rate was high because it was hard to find people who were committed enough to stay with the job after their earlier idealism had faded. The failures and problems were too high, the status and pay were too low.

During her four-year career Meredith had watched other probation officers leave the profession and determined that she would not be one of those who fell by the wayside. She had the dedication as well as the talent to succeed, and she had vowed that she would see it through. She knew from personal experience the difference a good probation officer could make. With a sigh Meredith thought of the pleasure she used to take in her work, even when the gains were slight. Her job used to give purpose and meaning to her life and help her keep other things in perspective.

Until Warren came along. And then she had let herself become so infatuated that everything else had become secondary to her desire for him. Waves of embarrassment rocked her as she remembered the television reporter who had asked such rude, impertinent questions about her "fast rise" from being a simple probation officer to being Director of Special Services.

Fast rise! Four years of working as hard as she could, using all her ingenuity to find ways to resolve problems and help her probationers make a new start in life. A promotion gained after four years of intense caring and doing in a job which was devoid of glamour, a promotion which was well-earned. And for that promotion to appear in the public eye as merely a trade-off in a romantic liaison distressed Meredith and cheapened her affair with Warren.

It had been so special, so wonderful. Warren was capable of such tenderness when he let himself go and stopped being a rational-thinking machine. How she longed for that tenderness again, and for the sensuality he aroused in her. But it could not be. She tightened her lips and stared at the sign on her new office door: "Director of Special Services." Everything had its price, she thought, but the cost of her new job seemed entirely too high if it meant she had to give up the man she loved.

But what other choice did she have? Even if she had turned down the new job and stayed a regular probation officer at the branch office, she and Warren were already a "public item," subject to suspicions where their work overlapped. The only way to keep Warren in her life would be to quit her job altogether and go into some other line of work. And that she could not do. She had too strong a sense of duty, too keen a desire to rescue damaged lives, to turn her back on her vocation. There was no other way.

And besides, Warren had never indicated that he wanted anything more than a casual affair. In fact, she thought wryly, he had been adamant that he did not want even a casual affair with her. He did not want her in his life at all. And could she blame him? One moment in the penetrating limelight of television had been enough for a lifetime. With all his years in the public eye, no wonder Warren valued circumspection. His relationship with Meredith had created a stir that rippled both their careers, just as he had predicted. But, damn it, why did he always have to be so right?

Knowing they had been right to part did not make it

any easier for Meredith. She was so full of pain that the slightest touch would have shattered her into a million pieces. Fortunately, the mind has ways of protecting itself, and when the pain became absolutely unbearable, her mind went numb—as though it had detached itself from its aching mass of flesh and watched with disinterest from above as Meredith went through the motions of living. Life had a certain sense of unreality while her mind was separated from her body, but at least she was able to function again. She kept other people at a distance so that hardly anybody got close enough to realize that her smile was only on her lips, not in her eyes, or that there was a perpetual tightness around her mouth. Meredith looked in the mirror as seldom as possible and tried to be grateful for the emotional paralysis which eased her suffering.

The lovely spring days turned to the sweltering heat of summer, and it suited Meredith to spend most of her spare time in the swimming pool at Barton Springs. She would go there straight from work and plunge into the cold, refreshing waters. She ignored the clusters of other people who frolicked around the pool, and soon they stopped asking her to join them. It was as though in the water she could be reborn, to wash away her despair and loss. Her numbness began to fade, leaving in its place a brittleness that had never been there before. She wondered if the hard line around her mouth was permanent. She knew she had changed, and not necessarily for the better, but she didn't know anything she could do about it.

And Warren? He did not call, not once. Their affair was no longer the object of the prying eyes of the world. No one had seen them together in weeks, not since that fateful day at the hospital, and thanks to Harvey, that gossipy tidbit never saw the light of day.

Currently there were other choice morsels of gossip for daily consumption: Warren was being seen more and more frequently with Bettis Langley, and there was idle speculation that perhaps this time Warren had met his match. Someone who swore to be privy to the truth claimed that they would marry at Christmas time.

Scott knew when he heard the story that he would have to tell Meredith, but to his relief she hardly reacted to the news. There was a look of momentary surprise on her face, and then she nodded. "That's fine," she said. "Bettis is very intelligent and savvy. They'll make a good couple."

"You're sure you don't mind?" Scott hated to probe an old wound, but he couldn't help wondering.

A gentle, sad smile played at the corners of Meredith's lips. "Why, no," she murmured. "My infatuation with Warren has been dead for a long time." She gazed upward into Scott's green eyes, so tender and full of concern. "You don't have to worry about me, Scott," she added, reaching out to pat his cheek.

They left the Old Pecan Street Cafe, where they had gone for a light, early dinner, and walked back down Sixth Street toward the capitol. Sixth Street was now bustling with its nighttime crowd of young professionals and university students, and along the way they bumped into various friends from the courthouse.

"Join us for a drink?" asked someone from the district attorney's office.

"Another time, thanks. I have some work to do at the office," Scott replied.

"Sure you do," responded the young prosecutor, with a sidelong glance at Meredith.

"For Pete's sake, Meredith and I are old friends," Scott sputtered. "Come on, Meredith, let me take you home where you'll be safe from lewd minds."

Everybody laughed, and Scott and Meredith went on their way. It was all so casual, so innocent, that it did not occur to either of them that before they even got to Congress Avenue, the story had begun to circulate that Scott and Meredith were "back together again" and trying to keep their romance a secret.

At her front door, Scott put his arms around Meredith and drew her nearer to him, then bent his head and pressed his lips to hers. In his kiss Meredith experienced a gentle, tender, unselfish *caring* that brought tears to her eyes.

"Oh, Scott, you're so sweet," she whispered. "I don't know what I would have done without you these past few weeks."

She could feel his smile spread through his body, and he hugged her close. "Do you mean that, Meredith?" he asked.

"Of course. You're my best friend."

"I want to be more than a friend, Meredith."

She looked into his eyes, her lip trembling. He bent his head to hers again.

There was no magic in Scott's kiss, no enchantment, no urgency, only a comfortable, reassuring warmth and affection. Meredith's lips were lifeless under Scott's. Was this the kind of kiss she would know for the rest of her days? But wasn't it better than the other kind, that kind that swept away everything in its path like a destructive flood? She choked back her tears. Yes, this was better, far better. Better to feel nothing than to feel too much.

Scott lifted his head and sighed. "It's no use, is it?"

"Scott, please," Meredith was remorseful. Scott was so dear, and she had not meant to hurt him. "I'm just . . . confused." She put her arm on his shoulder to caress him, but his hands stopped her.

"Look, Meredith, I know you too well. You can't fool old Scott."

"I wasn't trying to fool you," she answered in a muffled voice.

"Well, you were trying to fool yourself, then. But it just won't wash. I can't give you what you need any more than you can give me what I need."

"I'm sorry, Scott. You're the nicest guy in the world."

"Sure I am. But the chemistry just isn't there. We can't help that, can we?" He tilted her head and smiled into her eyes. If anything was bruised, it was his ego. His heart was still intact.

"Does this mean I won't see you again?" she asked, hating to give up an undemanding escort as well as a good friend.

"Heaven forbid. As much as you like. In fact, if you'll show me that dazzling smile of yours, I'll even let you come and watch me do my slow-pitch at the softball league tomorrow night."

Meredith smiled.

"That's better. Besides, I always pitch better when there's a good-looking woman to show off for."

In mid-August one of Scott's criminal cases was transferred to Dallas on a change of venue because of adverse pretrial publicity. It was a notorious case involving a prominent state official who had been indicted for perjury and misconduct, and who had money enough to pay Scott's firm very well for undertaking his defense. The senior partner of the firm would be the lead attorney, and Scott and another associate were to go with him to Dallas to assist with the trial. The trial was expected to last about three weeks, and the preparations would be intense. Scott was excited about the prospects of participating in a big case which would generate a lot of publicity. In his mind, a trial was as much of a spectacle as a football game, and the roar of a crowd made the combat more thrilling.

"You be sure to keep up with the softball team for me," Scott urged. "The guys give you all the credit for our winning streak."

"It's your pitching that did it, Scott. Everybody knows that. But I wouldn't miss a game for the world. There's nothing quite as entertaining as watching a bunch of courthouse jocks showing off their athletic prowess."

"But look how it's enhanced your reputation to be known as mascot of the Legal Eagles. You're the envy of every woman in town."

"Bettis Langley should be so lucky," Meredith answered, a twinkle in her eye.

On Saturday afternoon Meredith found herself too lonely and restless to sit still. She thought if she didn't get out of the house she would scream, and she flipped through the paper to consider some movie that would be sufficiently diverting. She noticed an advertisement for one of the special events at the University of Texas—a Renaissance Festival sponsored by the Fine Arts and Humanities departments—and decided that it would serve to pass the time. Meredith got in her car and drove over to the campus.

The courtyard between the Union and the West Mall Office Building was a spectacle of activity. There were booths set up everywhere selling food, soft drinks and beer, and the attendants were dressed in adaptations of Elizabethan costumes that looked like they had come straight off the cover of a Folger's edition of Shakespeare. Drama and music students took turns giving performances to an enthusiastic crowd made up not only of students but also of a good cross section of Austin's staunch supporters of the arts. A pretty red-haired serving wench flirted outrageously with a group of young, rugged males who responded with a proper appreciation of her charms.

Meredith couldn't understand why her heart felt so heavy when everybody else was having such a good time. She wandered through the bazaar admiring the jewelry and handcrafts made by students. At one booth a heavy gold chain intricately woven with topaz beads caught her eye.

"Would you like to try it on?" asked the student who supervised the booth, her voice hopeful. "The color would be perfect with your hair and eyes."

"Did you make it?" Meredith asked.

"Yes, it was my class project in summer school. Do you like it?"

"Oh, yes. It's quite beautiful," Meredith answered. "I'd love to have it." She needed something pretty and new to boost her spirits.

"Wonderful," the girl answered. "The necklace looks like it was made just for you."

Meredith found a shady spot under a tree and watched a group of dancers perform a lively English folk dance, the women dipping and swaying, their petticoats flying, as the men whirled them to and fro. Across the courtyard a lute player looking for all the world like Sir Walter Raleigh strummed a haunting melody. Propped against the stone buildings were ancient navigational maps showing the known world of the 1500's, and Meredith squinted in the sun, knowing that she would never find Austin, Texas, on any of those maps. What if America had never been discovered? she wondered. Would she have been born in another part of the world, someplace where she would never have met . . . ? She would not let herself finish the thought. It was too disturbing. Had it been fate for her to be in this place, at this time? She looked back at the red-haired wench, who was playfully pinching the cheek of a huge muscular youth who looked like he probably played left guard for the Texas Longhorns. Would it have turned out any differently if she and Warren had met in some other time, some other place? Would she have known a happy ending to her romance?

She was becoming morbid. She shook herself and got up to stroll around and mix with the crowd. Someone bumped her from behind, and she moved out of the way of a lanky man in jeans who had a portable video camera on his shoulder.

"Set up right here, Jack," called a feminine voice. "I think we can get most of it from that angle."

Meredith had not seen Bettis Langley since that morning at the hospital. To run into her suddenly and unexpectedly flustered Meredith. She stepped back, well out of camera range, while the crowd surged forward, eager to become part of a television news story.

It would not be just an ordinary story, Meredith could tell that at once. Bettis had given some careful thought to the subject of the Renaissance and made some perceptive comments before she turned to the audience and began asking questions.

"What do you think made Renaissance people different?" she asked a young history major.

"Their lust for life," he answered without hesitation. "They wanted to know all about everything; they were explorers, exploring the worlds of nature, science, language, and religion—" He was so caught up in the subject that he had a hard time expressing himself.

"The Renaissance man was the ideal . . . for *all* times."

"What do you mean by the Renaissance man?" asked Bettis.

"He embodied perfection in everything," exclaimed another student. "He was intelligent, and strong, and brave, a politician and a thinker, powerful . . ." The student paused to think and Bettis moved to someone else, asking the same question.

"—smart . . ."

"—literate . . ."

"—romantic . . ."

Meredith listened with interest to the descriptions that followed of this ideal man, a paragon of perfection, popular with men and irresistible to women. A picture of her own ideal man formed in her mind—Warren, with his dark eyes flaming with desire, his head tilted back, his arms outstretched. She blinked away the memory.

Bettis handed the microphone to someone else, a middle-aged, distinguished-looking gentleman. "This is Dean Holmes from the Law School," Bettis said, looking into the camera. "Tell us, Dean Holmes, you have some of the best minds in the country at your school. Do you know anyone who would qualify as a Renaissance man?"

The Dean smiled in amusement and stroked his chin. "That's a pretty tall order," he said. "But I guess if I had to pick just one of the students I've had over the years, it would be Warren Baxter. That list pretty much describes him." There was a burst of applause from an older group at the fringe of the crowd, and Meredith turned in surprise to see a group of politicians from the capitol, including the lieutenant governor, the attorney general . . . and an embarrassed-looking Warren Baxter. What on earth were they doing here at the University on a Saturday afternoon? Watching Bettis, Meredith quickly surmised why they were here. Bettis had planned the whole thing. Bettis knew what students would say when she asked them to describe a Renaissance man, so she found someone who would name Warren as that kind of man, and then conveniently had Warren on the spot. What appeared to be a completely spontaneous event was rigged, from beginning to end, by Bettis Langley. For a moment Meredith felt disgusted, but then the humor of it hit her. You had to admire a woman with that much ingenuity—or was it sheer *gall?*

Bettis trailed the cord to her microphone through the crowd and gave Warren a friendly smile. "Judge Baxter, you're being touted by your old law professor as a Renaissance man, and the university students have been telling our television audience what that means. I see you standing here with some of the most important men in the state, so that's proof that you're 'popular with men.' But what about being 'irresistible to women'?"

Warren had shaken off his embarrassment and was ready to enter into the frolicking atmosphere of the festival. Always the consummate politician, he gave a boyish grin and modestly lowered his eyes. "Aw, shucks, Bettis," he said, shuffling the ground with one foot.

"Everybody in Austin knows you're our No. 1 bachelor," Bettis continued. "How have you managed to stay single for so long?"

Warren's eyes crinkled in a grin that lit up television sets and assured him of an extra 7,000 votes in the next election. "Well, you know," he responded, dodging an elbow the lieutenant governor poked in his ribs, "there are so many beautiful women in Texas I could never pick out just one. But lately I've been thinking it might be nice to settle down."

"Really?" breathed Bettis, her voice coy. "How exciting! Who is the lucky girl?"

Warren winked at Bettis, his face creased with another engaging grin. "Why, Bettis, when I figure that out, you'll be the first to know."

Warren disappeared in a chorus of good-natured ribbing, and Bettis, her face flushed with success, wrapped up the newscast.

The crowd dispersed, to re-form around other novelties and entertainments. Meredith had had enough of the Renaissance Festival. She turned away from the West Mall and started across the tree-lined campus to the side street where she had parked her car. The crowd around her thronged toward a magician, and in the press of bodies she felt that she was trying to go the wrong way on a one-way street. Mockingbirds and cardinals chatted in the live oak trees overhead, aghast at this crowd which had taken over their peaceable domain.

"Meredith? Is that you?" inquired a male voice near at hand.

She turned. It was Warren, surprised to find her here.

"Hello, Warren." She paused in the crowd and fought to control her emotions. This time she *would* be poised. She nodded serenely, her face expressionless.

He took her arm and stepped aside from the crowd of people. "You're looking well," he said, taking note of her white Mexican ruffled blouse and blue prairie skirt. Her skin was tanned nearly as dark as his, and she was a picture of vitality and good looks.

"Thank you," she said, lowering her lashes. There

was no point in looking into his eyes. It would be disastrous for her thumping heart.

"Well . . . tell me how you've been," he said in the awkward pause. "I don't seem to run into you at the courthouse these days."

"No, my new job takes me out into the community. I don't have many occasions to go to the courthouse any more, just now and then to file something." They stood a moment wondering what to say next, and then they both spoke at once.

"How are things with you?" Meredith asked.

"Tell me about your job," Warren said simultaneously.

They laughed nervously. Neither could admit the leap of joy at the sight of the other. Both immediately pounded into submission their emotions and put on a façade of polite, courteous indifference. But the tension was there, and they both felt it.

"Maybe I ought to run on," Meredith said. "It wouldn't do to heat up the gossip again."

"Don't you know the best place to get lost is in a crowd? Nobody is paying any attention to us."

Meredith looked around. Everybody else was watching the magician. Still, she knew she should go. She could feel the crumbling of the defenses that had taken so long to erect. She gave Warren a bright, artificial smile and turned to leave. "Nice to see you again," she said.

"I'll walk you to your car," he said. "You still haven't told me how you like your new job." He fell into step beside her and they walked under a natural canopy of oak leaves as they passed the large stone buildings which dotted the campus.

"It's interesting. Much different from being a probation officer, and sometimes I really miss working with people on a one-to-one basis. But I'm working on some new programs, and I tell myself that I'm still helping people even if it's indirectly."

"Harvey gives us a report every month. He says you're doing a great job."

"Oh, well, you know Harvey. He was always my staunchest supporter."

They reached the open area of Littlefield Fountain, and Warren paused at the stone rail at the top of the steps. Nearby jets of water shot upward, spraying an Italian bronze sculpture of three sea horses, ridden by sea tritons, drawing winged Columbia in the Ship of State. Saying nothing, they gazed hypnotically at the water flowing from the statue back through a series of tiered pools. The terrible August heat beat down upon them, and finally Meredith said, "I really need to go. The sun is too hot this afternoon. I'm going to go take a swim and cool off."

"Barton Springs?"

"How did you know?"

"Word gets around."

"Now, why would anybody bother to repeat something so dull? What difference does it make where I swim?"

"You were quite a topic of conversation for a while," Warren said. "Everybody talked about how you went every day to Barton Springs but never said a word to anybody."

Meredith thought with a pang of that terrible time in the spring when she and Warren first parted. "I wasn't feeling very sociable then. But that was over two months ago. Surely nobody is talking about that now."

"The latest story has to do with baseball."

Meredith laughed. "Slow-pitch softball, to be correct. And yes, that is my newest diversion. Good for my tan," she added, glancing at her legs.

"The story is that *you're* the diversion."

"Not me. The guys have won the last ten games. They couldn't play like that if they were diverted."

"Maybe I should have said *inspiration* instead of diversion," Warren responded. He had heard the stories about Meredith and Scott getting back together and wanted to know whether it was true, without having to ask directly. It really was none of his business, but he had been curious for weeks. Meredith, however, refused to be smoked out. She could guess where his questions were heading and why. For her ego's sake she decided to let him believe the rumors were true about her relationship with Scott. For some reason it seemed terribly important to her that Warren think someone else loved her.

"Scott and I are . . . just friends," she said in a tremulous voice that insinuated just the opposite. She knew it was pride, but she did not want him to know how alone she really was. That was going to be her secret. She changed the subject. Now it was her turn.

"And how are things going with you, Warren? I noticed that Bettis was there to give you some nice publicity this afternoon."

He nodded. "Oh, I can always count on Bettis for that. Sometimes her stories are a little bit contrived, but for some reason the public enjoys them. I imagine I'll get fifty letters after the newscast tonight. And those who write letters usually remember to vote for me."

"The consummate politician."

"Oh, I do have a few battle scars."

"Just enough to make you interesting to the voters,"

she answered. "And with your own personal TV anchorwoman, she'll always present the scars in the most attractive light."

"It's not like you to be catty."

"Sorry. I thought I was being candid."

Warren grinned wryly to himself. Meredith was sometimes quite transparent. He was well aware of the rumors about himself and Bettis, but they were harmless rumors so he hadn't bothered to squelch them. In fact, *he* had been the one to start the rumor about a Christmas wedding. He had done it in order to deflect attention from the last-gasp stories about himself and Meredith. It was totally meaningless, and it amused him to have the last laugh on the talebearers. He had even told Bettis he had done it and since it could only enhance her career to have her name linked to his, she had even done her share of spreading the story. But that was their secret, and Warren had no intention of enlightening Meredith. Since she was now involved with Scott, Warren wanted her to know that he wasn't sitting home alone at night, either.

"Bettis and I go back a long way," he said. "She's covered my campaigns ever since I first ran for district attorney over at Bastrop. She's done me a lot of favors over the years."

Meredith's lips curved in a sparkling, though forced, smile. "How nice for both of you," she said cheerfully. She rose from the stone rail where she had been sitting. "It's been good to see you again, Warren, but I really must run." Then she added the Southern requisite to every farewell. "Do come by to see me sometime." Her words had the perfect ring of polite insincerity, and though her fingers touched his briefly, her eyes were averted. She was very proud of herself. She had finally played a role: she had hidden her real emotions and dealt with an awkward situation with poise and grace. Even Warren could not fault her composure.

She ran lightly down the steps and across the street to her car, waving a casual goodbye to Warren, who stood at the fountain without moving. Both of them were left wondering how the day could be so warm when the sun had disappeared into heavy clouds, leaving the earth in gloomy darkness.

Chapter Thirteen

Her chance meeting with Warren at the Renaissance Festival troubled Meredith. For a few days, feeling restless and trapped by circumstances, she considered quitting her job and going back to Houston. Finally she realized that she would not be any happier anywhere else; the unhappiness was inside her and would follow her wherever she went. There was no escape to be gained by running.

And she really did not know what she would be running from. Was it jealousy that Warren and Bettis were finding happiness together? Meredith would always love Warren, she recognized that now, but the demands of her work were in conflict with the demands of his. Neither of them could meet their professional responsibilities and function properly when their personal lives and emotions became so tangled up in their work.

And Meredith could not give up her work. It was too important to her. Somehow it was part of her identity, her very self, and to give it up would be to destroy the very thing that made her *herself,* uniquely Meredith Jennings. In a way she envied women who could turn their backs on the professional world and find their whole identity in the role of wife and mother, but Meredith could not join the ranks of those women. While she, too, wanted to be a wife and mother, it could not be at the price of giving up her life's work. Maybe if she had never been arrested in Houston all those years ago . . . maybe if she had never become a probation officer and learned to help people in need, but those things had happened to her and had made her into the woman she now was. If those things had not happened, she would be a different woman today. A different woman would be free to make another decision, and perhaps would make a different decision. But *this* Meredith Jennings could not.

The changes that had taken place in Meredith's life in recent weeks had matured her and made her more thoughtful and reflective. She lost most of the self-righteousness that had marked her earlier career because she was no longer sure she was right every time. Colleagues who had previously admired and respected her but kept a safe distance now found that she could actually laugh at herself and have fun. Her probationers found, to their surprise, that she had lost the tendency to indulge them and make excuses for their failings. She could finally recognize that probationers were not necessarily helpless victims and that some of them could not be rehabilitated, no matter how hard the supervising probation officer might try to help them.

These changes came gradually while Meredith struggled with her inner conflicts and came to a better understanding of herself. In time she was able to forgive herself for her mistakes and give credit for her successes. At that point, she finally was free, and then she no longer needed to think of quitting her job and moving to another city. She was at peace within, and so she could be at peace in Austin, Texas, even if Warren Baxter lived there, too, and married Bettis Langley.

Or could she? No matter how hard Meredith tried to resign herself to her lonely life and find satisfaction in helping other people, her love for Warren remained, permeating her existence. She ran into him occasionally, but her feelings did not fluctuate depending on whether he smiled at her or not, as they had in the old days of her infatuation with him, now that she had admitted to herself that she loved him, that love became bedrock in her heart, steadfast and unchanging. For her own good, she tried determinedly to douse any lingering thoughts of Warren, but there was no way she could put an end to the love she had for him.

Meredith had gone on a rare trip to the courthouse to file some papers in the district clerk's office when Scott telephoned her office early on the morning of his return from Dallas. Too excited to wait for her to get back, he hurried from his office in the bank building to the courthouse and met her at the third-floor foyer. "Meredith!" he shouted, oblivious of the attorneys and law clerks who were beginning to gather for the September docket call. She turned to him in glad surprise, for she had missed him during the three weeks he was in Dallas trying his case.

"You must have won your case," she said. "I've never seen you so happy."

"Won the case? Oh, yes, we did. But I didn't run up three flights of stairs to tell you that."

Meredith waited in anticipation for him to get words past the big smile that split his face. "Then what is it, Scott?"

"Meredith, do you believe in love at first sight?" The smile lit his body until she could almost see sparks fly off him.

"What?"

"Meredith, the most wonderful thing has happened," he said. "I met the most terrific woman in Dallas and we're going to get married!"

"Married! Oh, Scott, that's wonderful!" Meredith cried, throwing herself into Scott's outstretched arms. He grabbed her in a bear hug, then kissed her noisily. "Married! Meredith, I'm the luckiest man in the world!" In their shared joy, they did not see Warren step out of the elevator and walk past just in time to see their embrace and hear their final words.

Though Meredith had pondered the role of fate in her life, it was Scott who experienced that mysterious, fickle, chance encounter with destiny. He had gone to Dallas on a routine trip, totally devoid of adventure, his mind on nothing but winning his lawsuit. And there, in the most unromantic of places—the county courthouse—while scrambling from one office to another trying to gain access to a photocopier, he had met Tracy Caldwell, an impish, gamin-faced assistant district attorney with a playful, humorous streak that surpassed his own.

Scott suddenly found his days full of anticipation, wondering what she would do next.

Tracy seemed to know from the first moment that Scott was the man she had been waiting for, a kind of recognition in her sparkling blue eyes that staked him out as her own private territory. Her love, which had been held in trust for twenty-seven years, now found its object and spilled over as fresh and pure as an underground stream. For Scott, to be loved so totally, so selflessly, and so thoroughly was a new experience. He had spent two years convincing himself that he was in love with Meredith, always fearful and anxious that his love would never be reciprocated, trying to content himself with giving more than he would ever receive from her. To be on the receiving end of a loving relationship was an intoxicating experience, and before the week was out, Scott knew that everything he could possibly want from life was his in the fiery-haired, sparkling-eyed assistant district attorney of Dallas County.

He realized, though, that it would take time to work out their separate careers, and he thought it might be wiser to wait for a year before they got married. When he suggested that to Tracy, however, she snorted with indignation.

"When are you supposed to go back to Austin?" she asked, her red curls bouncing.

"As soon as this case is over," he answered, drooping.

"And when do you go to court in Austin?"

"As soon as I get back. I have a civil case on the September docket."

"And how long will it be before you have all your cases out of the way?" she asked, her lips in a crisp line.

"I don't know, Tracy. Months, maybe."

Tracy's blue eyes rolled heavenward and she drummed the table with her fingernails.

Scott swallowed hard. "But, Tracy . . ."

Tracy sat up straight. It was so *simple*—they could get married and *then* work out the details about their careers. "Scott, you could ask the judge for a continuance on one of your cases so we can get married. If you really *want* to get married, that is. This is a decision that nobody can make but you. But when you do, I want you to ask yourself if anybody else loves you the way *I* love you?"

Scott's face was stricken. Nobody had ever loved him the way Tracy did.

He did not have to say a word, Tracy could read the answer in his eyes. Not for nothing was she a prosecutor. She closed in for the kill. "And do you love *me* the way I love *you?"*

"Tracy! Have mercy!"

She rose, her tiny frame a dynamo of compressed energy with lightning-quick movements. "I'm leaving, Scott, and I think it will be best if we don't see each other again until you make up your mind. I wouldn't want to influence your decision." Before he could kiss her goodbye, she was gone.

Judge Baxter's courtroom was crowded with people at the September docket call. In the corners small groups of lawyers talked earnestly, trying to settle cases before the judge called them for trial. Other lawyers watched the comings and goings and tried to guess the number of cases that would actually settle. At docket call a case at the bottom of the list can suddenly find itself at the top because everything in between has folded. Witnesses have to be in telephone reach so they can be called on short notice. To be a trial lawyer requires nerves of steel and the mental agility to cope with rapidly changing circumstances. Still, lawyers who thrive on trial law feel a certain condescension toward "paper lawyers" who stay in the office all day with a fixed routine. At docket call the friendly conviviality of a special breed prevailed, relaxed and bantering, but whose adrenalin would surge when the action started.

"All rise," cried the bailiff, and everybody scrambled to attention. Court was in session.

Seven cases ahead of Scott's had been called, and all had announced ready. If they were all tried, they would fill the September term and his case would not be reached. If one of them settled before its trial date, though, it would leave space for him. He puzzled over the logistics as Warren called his case.

"Your Honor, plaintiff announces ready for trial—"

"That's fine, counsel. I'll list you as first alternate if one of the cases ahead of you settles at the last minute." Warren peered at his copy of the docket sheet and made some pencil notations.

"Your Honor?"

Warren turned his attention to Scott. "Do you have a problem, counsel?"

"Well, not exactly, Your Honor, but I was wondering . . ." Scott paused, trying to think how to proceed. Docket call was a little more informal than most other court sessions, and lawyers could usually approach the judge with a certain amount of candor. It was to everybody's benefit to work out an efficient docket schedule, and that meant lawyers had to explain trial settings in other courts and any personal conflicts.

Warren waited. He forced himself to be patient and tried to forget that a scant hour ago, out in the courthouse lobby, he had seen Meredith in Scott's arms.

"Well, Your Honor, you see, I'd like to try this case if we could do it in the September term, but it's going to make a problem for me if it gets passed and carried over to the October term."

"But, counsel, you know there's no way I can guarantee that one of the cases ahead of you will settle and make room for you. And if we don't reach you, then you'll be carried over."

"Well, Judge, that's the problem. I mean, I'm going to get married early in October, and I don't want to have to come back from my honeymoon to try this case."

There was laughter from the other lawyers, and someone clapped Scott on the back. There was general agreement that a honeymoon was no time to try a lawsuit, and everybody turned expectantly to the judge.

Warren managed a thin smile and nodded. "Very well," he agreed. "If we don't reach your case this term, we'll reset it for November. Will that give you enough time for your honeymoon?"

The courtroom laughter became more ribald, and red-faced, Scott agreed that a month would be an adequate time. Warren called the next case and tried not to notice that the world was caving in around him. By the time docket call was over, his face was gray and he hurried from the courtroom back to his office, with a sharp word to Miss Tuttle to hold his calls. His right hand gently massaged the left side of his chest as though it could ease his aching heart.

He had rejected all the rumors because he could not believe that Meredith would actually marry Scott. How could she? She loved *him,* Warren. Nobody knew that better than he did. It was written all over her face every time he saw her. Marry Scott? That young, good-looking, bronzed *softball pitcher!* Warren leaned his head against his hand. Somehow he had to find the dignity to get through this unexpected blow. He reached for the telephone. He had to call Meredith. That was it. He had to call and congratulate her. He would do the correct thing. It was what he had disciplined himself to do for his entire adult life. He dialed her number. If he had a momentary, desperate thought that she might change her mind when she heard his voice, he did not allow himself to put the thought into words. No, he would do the correct thing and extend his best wishes. And send a handsome gift. But he would not go to the wedding.

"Miss Jennings, please," he said when the receptionist answered the telephone at the probation office. "To San Marcos? Oh, I see. . . . When do you expect her back? . . . Is there anywhere I can reach her? . . . No, nothing urgent. . . . Please tell her that Warren Baxter called. I'll return the call later."

He returned the receiver to its cradle and with excruciating politeness requested that Miss Tuttle bring him a cup of very hot, very black, coffee. He spent the rest of the day isolated in his office staring at a law book without even realizing that it was upside down.

The news of Scott's engagement to Tracy quickly made the rounds, but it was hours before Warren heard it. Unfortunately, Miss Tuttle did not gossip and thus was not privy to the tidbits of news about the courthouse regulars who were the frequent topic of conversation among the court clerks, secretaries, bailiffs and janitors. This was her only real failing as a secretary.

As a matter of fact, Warren learned the news only by accident. He overheard Jo Betsy, the deputy clerk, discussing the engagement with one of the secretaries at quitting time that night while they were all waiting for the elevator. He turned on his heel, marched straight back to his office, and picked up the telephone.

"Has Meredith Jennings returned to the office?" he asked the irritable receptionist who had been detained by the ringing of the telephone.

"I don't think so."

"Would you please check?"

"We-ee-ll." She was obviously reluctant. Her husband was waiting downstairs with the kids.

"This is Judge Baxter."

The receptionist did not walk, she ran, through the hallway to Meredith's empty office. "Sorry, Judge," she said, breathless, returning to the telephone.

"Do you know whether she's coming back to the office today?"

"Sorry. She didn't say."

"Thank you for your trouble." Warren slammed down the receiver and jutted his chin against his fist. He was finding it impossible to think with this strange roaring in his ears. Where could she be? Did she go home? Did she meet someone? And most of all, *was it true?* For the entire miserable day he had believed that Meredith and Scott were going to be married. He had seen them in each other's arms, then Scott had asked for a continuance so he could take a honeymoon . . .

But that honeymoon was not to be with Meredith. Scott was engaged to a lady-lawyer from Dallas . . . *maybe.* If true, then the stories about Meredith and Scott had been as false as the stories about himself and Bettis. But Meredith herself had insinuated that she and Scott were—think, Baxter, come on—why had she let him think there was more to it than there was?

He put his head in his hands and sighed. Probably for the same reason he had let her think there was something between himself and Bettis. Meredith had been so cool, so poised that day at the Renaissance Festival, that he had believed her words rather than the look in her eyes. Be honest with yourself, Baxter, he thought. You always knew her love was there for the asking but you wouldn't ask.

He walked to the window and stared out at the oaks and pecan trees, their leaves drenched golden in the late afternoon sun. Where was the solution to the mystery of Meredith? She was an unfathomable riddle that he would never understand. No matter how well he might know her, there was something elusive about her that beckoned like fog just beyond his reach.

And then he remembered the dream that had haunted him for weeks. He could not understand Meredith because he would not let himself; he would not untie the silk handkerchief that bound his mouth and kept him from calling her back to him. He was afraid of her. Afraid of her sheer exuberance, her openness, her willingness to give without counting the cost. She threatened his need to keep life—and people—in tidy little compartments. She complicated things for him because she insisted on a life that was all of a piece, without his partitions. He had never asked for her love because he was afraid of what it would cost him to love in return.

He could not cross the barriers that separated them with his intellect. But it was his heart that cried out for her, that stern, well-disciplined heart that he had long ago locked into a cupboard until Meredith, with her tempestuous spirit, had flung open the door and warmed him with the sunlight of her love.

In his heart Warren found his answer. Perhaps he would never understand Meredith; but no matter how much he had hurt her, or how much she had hurt him, they loved one another. He was suddenly as sure of his own love as he was of hers. An astonished smile broke across his face. He tossed aside his briefcase and loped out the door.

Meredith had driven back from San Marcos in the 91-degree heat with no air conditioning in her Volkswagen and was drenched with perspiration by the time she got home. She picked up the newspaper from the front porch, riffled through the day's collection of junk mail and bills, and decided a shower had first priority on the evening's agenda. She took off her cotton khaki suit and tossed it with the clothes that needed to be taken to the drycleaner, then went into the bathroom and turned on cool water for her shower. She would have welcomed Barton Springs on this unseasonably warm September day. When she had stayed under long enough to cool off, she climbed out, towel-dried her hair, and squirmed into a butternut-colored halter and a pair of white shorts that emphasized the bronze tan she had acquired during the summer months at Barton Springs. She casually flipped on the television set in the living room and wandered back into the kitchen to pour herself a tall glass of iced tea.

Her little house seemed unbearably hot, so Meredith got the newspaper and her glass of tea and went out to the backyard to lie under the pecan tree in a hammock. She lay there half-asleep, too lazy even to look at the paper, listening to the blue jays scolding a trespassing starling. Eventually she propped herself up on one elbow and brushed her hair until it dried, then lay back again, sipping her tea and daydreaming. She ought to think about preparing something for supper, but the heat had ruined her appetite and anyway, she was too sluggish to move.

She was almost asleep when she became aware of a car roaring down the quiet neighborhood street. She rolled over in the hammock and pulled a pillow over her head, but still she could hear the tires squealing on the hot pavement. Apparently the car stopped nearby because the street suddenly became quiet again. Lazily Meredith rolled out of the hammock and walked to the gate, but she couldn't tell where the car had stopped. She went back inside, but before she had time to pour herself another glass of iced tea, there was an urgent rapping at her front door.

"Meredith!" called Warren.

"Warren?" she cried, throwing open the wooden door. The expression on his handsome face was so intense she stopped dead in her tracks, staring at him, while her heart turned over with joy.

"May I come in?" he asked politely.

Flustered, she stepped out of the way so he could come inside. What did that expression mean? He looked as if at any moment he might possibly devour her. Meredith suddenly became aware of her scanty halter and shorts and began backing slowly away from him.

He grinned that devilish grin that lit up his eyes and made little wrinkles at the creases and a dimple twitched at the corner of his mouth. With each step Meredith took backward, he took another, stalking her. She found herself bumping up against the wall with no more room to retreat. His body closed against hers, pressing her completely against the wall. He leaned his arms against the wall at either side of her head, imprisoning her. She was aware of nothing but his warm breath against her face, his fiery eyes boring into her. She demurely dropped her eyelids. It would not do for him to read her thoughts at this moment.

"One question," he said, his voice urgent against her ear. She nodded her head. "Is it true that Scott Palmer is going to marry a lady-lawyer from Dallas?" She nodded again. "Meredith Jennings!" he cried. "I ought to whale you for the worry I've had today!" A wicked light gleamed in his eye. "As a matter of fact . . ." he murmured.

"Warren, *no!*" Meredith shrieked, struggling to free herself from the makeshift prison of his arms.

"Hold still," he said, pressing her closer against the wall. Goose bumps raced down her spine at the contact with the exciting strength of his lean, hard body.

"Warren, I can't breathe," she whispered against the hollow of his shoulder.

"Serves you right," he said, lifting her face to the air with strong, brown fingers. "Do you have any idea the hell I've been through?"

Meredith could not look at him when there was so much raw pain in his eyes. She thought of her own hell and wondered if he could read it in her eyes the way she did his.

"I don't know why it took me so long to figure out that the rumors about you and Scott were untrue," he said, brushing her cheek with a tender kiss, his voice still full of pain and wonder. There was a choking sensation in Meredith's throat. She had never realized that the stories might have hurt him. He was so self-assured, and he had Bettis Langley to console him.

His lips brushed her forehead, her eyelids, her fingertips. His lips trailed down her neck. She trembled in his arms, as his lips roamed over her temples, back down her cheek to her quivering chin. She could smell tobacco and soap as he nuzzled her neck, and shaving lotion, and desire . . . and regret. Her heart burst with love and she clasped her arms around his neck. "Oh, Warren, darling. I'm so sorry you misunderstood."

Her kisses fell against his shirt, his neck, his hands.

His fingers caught in her thick golden hair and pulled back her head, but she dared not look into his eyes. His mouth fell upon hers, greedy for her response. His lips parted, his tongue begged her forgiveness. He lifted her in his arms, straining her against him, and walked to the rocking chair. He sat down, holding her close in his arms.

"We have to talk about it sooner or later," he said. In an attempt to control the emotions that churned within him, he took a packet of cigarettes from his breast pocket and knocked one loose, then tapped it against the arm of the chair. His fingers were trembling, and Meredith reached out and traced the outline of his palm. He struck a match and lit the cigarette with a sharp intake of breath. He leaned back and exhaled slowly, his free hand gently caressing Meredith's bronzed leg. She bent her head close to his and gently nibbled his ear. He smiled down at her.

"That isn't going to work, you know," he said, his voice husky. "It's only a temporary distraction." Her fingers traced his dark eyebrows, his cheekbones, his nose, then lingered to trace, ever so slowly, the pulsing outline of his lips.

He blew smoke in her face.

"Warren!" she protested, twisting away her head.

"Behave yourself," he instructed putting out his cigarette. "It's time we worked out our differences. We can't talk when you're so damned seductive."

She attempted to rise from his lap but he caught her wrist in his strong fingers. "Ouch," she whimpered. He lifted her wrist to his lips and rained baby kisses on it.

"All better now?"

She nodded.

His fingers pressed against her bare back and toyed with the strings to her halter. She blushed and sat up straight in his lap.

"Tell me why you gave up on me," he whispered. She made the mistake of taking a peek at him, and when she saw his ravaged face, her heart broke.

"Oh, Warren, I was so stupid," she cried. "I wouldn't listen to you about the gossip. You tried to tell me—and then we nearly got our careers ruined—and it would have happened if Harvey hadn't been there, and it never would have happened if only I'd listened to you and there's—"

"Hey, hey, take it easy," he crooned, pulling her head against his chest. "Take your time."

"I know you were right and I should have listened, but Warren, you're not always right and I have my job to do, too, and it's just as important as yours even if it doesn't have as much status because sometimes I help people, you know I do, and Warren, I have to keep helping them, honest, I have to, I owe it to Mrs. Dickinson, and if I didn't keep *working,* I wouldn't be *me,* can't you understand?—" Her face was contorted with pain, but Warren was completely bewildered. What on earth did any of this have to do with *them?*

"Meredith, please slow down. I don't have the faintest idea what you're talking about."

Meredith, who was gasping for breath, looked at the blank expression on his face in total surprise. She had always thought he was brilliant, but she had been wrong. He was downright dumb. She started over, explaining it very slowly so he could not fail to understand.

He listened quietly while she told him in very short,

simple sentences why their relationship was impossible due to his duties as a judge and hers as a probation officer. Her chin quivering, she explained that she could not give up her work any more than he could give up his. Even though he had said the same thing to himself a thousand times, he suddenly realized that such logic must have come straight from outer space. Why hadn't he realized earlier that their problem could be resolved? The gossip which had tortured them would have meant nothing if only he had been willing to make a commitment to their relationship—but he had been afraid, so afraid that he had nearly lost the most precious thing in life. He pulled Meredith close against his chest and held her so tightly she could hardly breathe.

"Warren?" she whispered, her words muffled.

He tilted her face and kissed her hair, her eyes. His lips wandered, seeking hers, but she turned her head away.

"Warren, you haven't told me what you're thinking yet," she said insistently.

He placed his hands on her face and pulled it near to his own, his dark eyes smoldering with lazy fires. His lips found hers and moved with an urgent pressure, demanding her response. Shivers of delight raced up her spine as he drank her sweetness in a kiss that lasted so long her senses reeled. When he finally drew away, her breath was as ragged as his.

"Does that answer your question?" he asked with an impudent grin.

"Not quite," she answered, her breath still coming fast.

"Then let me explain myself in a little more detail," he murmured in a husky voice. Again his lips claimed hers, warm and sweet, promising everything, withholding nothing. In this kiss was more than passion. There were tenderness and affection as well, sharing and caring . . . and love.

"Great heavens!" Warren cried, jumping up and dumping Meredith unceremoniously from his lap. "How could I have been so blind?" He gazed at her in stupefaction, then glanced at the antique clock on the wall. It was ten minutes to six.

"What's wrong?" Meredith wondered if Warren had lost his mind. There was a very strange look in his eyes. She rubbed her bottom where she had landed on the floor.

Warren grabbed the telephone. "Get me Bettis Langley," he shouted to someone at Channel 36. "Only thing to do is fight fire with fire," he mumbled to himself while he waited. ". . . tell the whole damn world, only way to put a stop to the whispers . . . *Bettis!* Listen to me, I told you that you could have the scoop when I decided—what? You're going where? . . . well, do me one last favor, will you?" He began to talk very rapidly while Meredith eavesdropped, her mouth agape.

When he hung up the telephone, he turned back to Meredith and found her smiling with delight, though her eyes were sparkling with tears.

"I'm sorry you had to hear it second-hand, but there wasn't time to ask you first," he said, with only a slightly apologetic tone. "Come here and let me do it properly."

Meredith melted into his arms and lifted her face for his kiss.

"Just a minute—I forgot the flowers," Warren said, hurrying from the room while Meredith stood there, face uptilted and eyes closed, wondering what was going to happen next. He was back in an instant with a large bouquet of red roses wrapped in green florist tissue. "I left them outside, just in case you were going to marry Scott," he explained, handing her the roses with a boyish smile. "There aren't any bluebonnets this time of year. Now," he said, sounding a little self-conscious and suddenly very, very shy. He pulled Meredith into his arms, roses and all, and gazed into her soft, brown eyes. "Miss Jennings, will you do me the honor of becoming my wife?"

"Well . . ." Meredith paused and tapped her forefinger against her chin, her brow furrowed as though in enormous concentration.

"Meredith!" Warren yelped. "It's going to be on TV any second. *Tell me!*"

"Haven't you forgotten something important?" she said, refusing to be hurried.

Warren dropped to his knees and reached for her hand. "I never dreamed you'd expect me to do this!" he muttered.

Meredith giggled. "Not that, silly." She dropped onto the floor beside him.

"Then what? If you don't hurry, we're going to miss the newscast."

Now it was Meredith's turn to be shy. She lowered her lashes and whispered, "Aren't you supposed to say something to me about love?"

Warren smiled. "Oh, you darling goose. Would I be down here on the floor like this if I didn't?"

"Well, a woman needs to hear it, you know." She lifted her eyes to his. He had never, never said that he loved her, and her heart longed to hear those words.

He swallowed past the lump in his throat. A lifetime of holding his emotions in check caught up with him. He pulled her close to him, but the words would not come. He tried to speak, but only a strangled cough escaped his lips. A sense of panic rose in him. Why couldn't he say it?

Meredith's brown eyes watched him expectantly, but with his silence her expression turned to dismay. Then she peered into his eyes and saw his desperation. Her warm heart flooded with compassion. The love was there in his eyes, but he could not voice it.

She clasped her arms around his neck and moved her face so close to his that their noses almost touched. "My darling, darling Warren, I love you with all my heart, and nothing would make me happier than to become your wife." She offered her lips for his kiss, and he swept her into his arms.

"Meredith, Meredith," he whispered, kissing her face, her neck, her shoulders. "I've never known anyone like you." His lips traveled back to hers, eager for the liquid fire of her kiss, the pulsing warmth of her tongue against his. She kissed him with total abandon, filled with a wild and raging passion borne of her love, willing to give not only her body but her very self. Her surrender was so total, her trust in him so complete, that it swept away the barriers of reserve that Warren could not overcome by himself. He lifted his head and gently clasped her face in his hands. She was so beautiful with her skin glowing with desire, her golden hair fragrant.

Would he someday gaze into a miniature of Meredith's beloved face in a child of their own? Not a red, squalling nonentity like those *other* babies in the hospital, but *their* child, born of *their* love? His eyes caressed Meredith's features, so beautiful, so precious to him. How stupid he had been to fear the responsibility of commitment—and how lucky not to have lost her forever. The love he had denied for so long welled up inside until he thought he would burst, and with a groan he caught her to his chest. "My darling, I love you, I love you, I love you," he murmured over and over. When they kissed again, each could taste the salt of the other's tears and neither was ashamed.

"Warren, we're going to miss the news," Meredith murmured at last.

"Who cares?" he responded, pulling her onto his lap.

"I do," she said, shaking her head to clear it and trying to focus her eyes. "Let me turn up the sound."

"We've already missed it," he said, catching her arm.

"It wouldn't have been the first story," she insisted, leaning across him to turn the dial. Filled with utter, blissful contentment, she curled back into Warren's arms and reached for the roses, burying her head in their fragrance.

There was so much local news that Bettis Langley was barely able to crowd in a story about Warren, and while Bettis reported the day's political events and the latest environmental squabble, Warren busied himself with kissing Meredith until she was breathless. By sheer coincidence they came up for air just as Bettis mentioned Warren's name.

"Channel 36 learned only minutes ago that Judge Warren Baxter is resigning his position as state district judge in order to run for the vacancy on the state supreme court left by the recent death of Judge Crownover. Judge Baxter told this reporter that he was resigning for personal reasons. He plans to marry Meredith Jennings, a former probation officer who is now Director of Special Services, and Judge Baxter wants to avoid any possible conflict of interest concerning their positions. Judge Baxter and Miss Jennings will be married in a public ceremony next month at the Oriental Gardens at Zilker Park.

"And now, ladies and gentlemen, thank you for

joining us tonight. This is the final broadcast of my career in Austin. On Monday I start a new job with a TV station in Washington, D.C., where I will be covering national politics. Goodnight . . . and goodbye."

Bettis smiled directly into the camera, but Warren and Meredith did not see. They were in each other's arms, kissing with a sweet passion that swept away every adversity.

Coming Next Month

Love's Gentle Chains by Sondra Stanford

Lynn had fled from Drew believing she didn't belong in his world. Then she discovered she was bound to him by her love and the child he had unknowingly fathered.

All's Fair by Lucy Hamilton

Automotive engineer Kitty Gordon had been in love with race driver Steve Duncan when she was sixteen. But this time, she would find the inside track to his heart.

Love Feud by Anne Lacey

Carole returned to the hills of North Carolina and rediscovered Jon. His family was still an anathema to hers, but he drew her to him with a sensuous spell she was unable to resist.

Cry Mercy, Cry Love by Monica Barrie

Heather Strand, although blind since birth, saw more clearly than Reid Hunter until love sharpened his vision and he realized that Heather was the only woman for him—forever.

A Matter Of Trust by Emily Doyle

After being used by one man, Victoria Van Straaten wanted to keep Andreas at arm's length. However, on a cruise to Crete she found Andreas determined to close the distance.

Dreams Lost, Dreams Found by Pamela Wallace

It was as though Brynne was reliving a Scottish legend with Ross Fleming—descendant of the Lord of the Isles. Only this time the legend would have a happy ending.